JENNIFER LI SHOTZ

#1 *New York Times* bestselling author

HARPER

An Imprint of HarperCollins*Publishers*

Scout: Firefighter

Produced by Alloy Entertainment
1325 Avenue of the Americas
New York, NY 10019

Library of Congress Control Number: 2018948003
ISBN 978-0-06-280261-3 (paperback)
ISBN 978-0-06-280250-7 (hardcover)
ISBN 978-0-06-288989-8 (paper-over-board)
18 19 20 21 22 CG/LSCH 10 9 8 7 6 5 4 3 2 1

First Edition

*For Por Por and Violet, who taught me
the importance of being kind*

1

SCOUT SEEMED TO KNOW THAT THE crowd had come to see him. He puffed out his chest and rotated his big, pointy ears to the front of his head. His brown-and-white fur had been shampooed and brushed for the occasion, making him look dignified and serious instead of goofy and eager, like he usually did. His brown eyes glittered playfully under the stage lights.

He was a handsome mutt, and he looked extra proud in his shiny new K-9 National Guard vest, stitched with an American flag and his name in capital letters: SCOUT.

The dog shifted from one paw to the other, trying hard to obey the sit command he'd been given.

Matt knew what Scout *really* wanted to do. He

wanted to hop to his feet, wag his tail wildly in the air, and prance around the room, sniffing at everyone. If dogs could smile, Matt knew Scout would be grinning from ear to ear.

But Scout was a good dog, and he was doing what good dogs do. He had been told to sit, so he sat. With his head cocked to the side, Scout focused on Matt's mom, Colonel Tackett, who stood next to him onstage and spoke to the audience.

Colonel Tackett was beaming as she welcomed Scout to the National Guard K-9 unit of Nevada. Finally, after months of training and a dangerous rescue mission, Scout was officially on the job.

Matt's mom held up Scout's certificate for the audience of servicemen and -women to see.

"And now, for the dog of the hour," she said. "May I present to you my friend Scout."

Matt let out a wild cheer, but he was drowned out by his older sister Bridget's "woo-hoo!" and his new friend Dev's piercing whistle. The crowd around them burst into raucous applause. As they hooted and hollered, Matt and Scout made eye contact. At the sight of Matt, Scout bobbed his head and let out a silent woof, then swished his tail across the ground.

Matt's mom laughed and waited for everyone to quiet down.

"I think every single person here today knows how I feel about Scout." She winked at Matt, and Matt felt the eyes of the entire room on him.

"Scout saved my kids' and their friends' lives. That is something a mother never forgets. So, I'm honored to say that Scout has finished his training and is now a certified member of the National Guard." She squatted down next to Scout and put her hands on the sides of his head. Scout sniffed at her face, and Matt's mom scratched him under the chin. She whispered something to him, and Scout licked her on the cheek.

Matt's mom stood up. Her eyes were a little damp, and she brushed away a tear. She cleared her throat. "And I'd also like to thank my son, Matt Tackett."

Matt's eyebrows shot up in surprise—he hadn't expected her to say that. His mom smiled broadly at him, her eyes still dewy, and Bridget elbowed him in the ribs.

"Awww," Bridget exhaled, so softly only Matt could hear. "Who's the hero now?"

Matt elbowed her back but kept a straight face. He suddenly became hyperaware of his stiff new shirt and the weird way his hair was slicked down and neatly brushed. It was a strange feeling to have a whole crowd of people staring at him.

"My son," his mom went on, "saw something in Scout that—I won't lie—I didn't see at first. But Matt and Scout *understood* each other. Matt knew that Scout needed time and encouragement to become the dog he was meant to be. So, Matt, this honor is as much for you as it is for Scout."

Matt's face went hot. He looked around sheepishly and gave an awkward little wave at the assorted trainers and K-9 specialists who were, much to his embarrassment, still staring at him.

He hated being the center of attention, but he sure couldn't argue with his mom when it came to Scout—and the bond they had.

When Scout had arrived in Nevada, Matt's mom had wanted to ship him right back to where he had come from. She didn't think he had what it took to be a highly skilled search-and-rescue dog.

Matt had begged her not to send Scout back, and he'd even surprised himself with how upset he was about it. But Matt had been upset about a lot of things back then—from his family's sudden move to Silver

City, to the need to make new friends *again*, to the fact that his dad, a first sergeant, was on a long deployment to Afghanistan.

Something about Scout had helped Matt start to feel better. He had seen how special Scout was from day one. Matt knew, from his own experience, that when you're the new guy in town, people often don't see you for who you really are. Just like Matt, Scout needed a friend to believe in him.

Matt had decided to train Scout in secret, hoping that he could convince his mom to keep the dog in her K-9 program. But before they could make any real progress, a dam broke and flooded their town.

That's when Scout proved himself all on his own. The instant the flood hit, he transformed from a nervous pup to an unbelievably brave dog. He jumped into action, saving Matt, Bridget, Dev—and even some strangers too.

Now there was no doubt in anyone's mind: Scout was heroic beyond their wildest hopes.

And though he was technically Colonel Tackett's dog—well, the National Guard's dog—no one could tear him away from Matt. Scout had become Matt's shadow, following him around the house, whining when Matt left for school, and waiting for him by the front door when he came home. Scout was part best friend and part fierce protector, and Matt felt the same way about his dog.

Matt and Scout would do anything for each other.

They were a team.

2

"MORNING, SUNSHINE!" Someone smacked Matt hard on the back.

"Morning, Dev." Matt grinned without turning around. He didn't need to look to know who it was. He could recognize that voice—and that painful hello—with his eyes closed.

Matt snapped his bike lock shut and readjusted the heavy backpack on his shoulders. The late-spring day was already getting hot, and the morning sun glinted off the windows of their two-story school building. Parts of the school were still under repair—the entire first floor had been totally destroyed by the flood. It had taken weeks for the building to dry out, but things

7

were finally starting to feel back to normal—just in time for summer vacation.

It was hard for Matt to believe, but he only had a month left of sixth grade.

"Hi, Matt."

At the sound of a girl's voice, Matt suddenly became aware of the root of every single hair on his head. He spun around to see Amaiya leaning against the end of the bike rack. Her long brown hair was pulled back in braids, and the freckles on her nose were pronounced in the sunlight.

"Hey, Amaiya!"

"Good morning, Ms. Amaiya," Dev said, tipping his head in her direction with a little flourish of his hand. "How are you this fine day?"

"I'm fine, dork."

"I don't believe *I'm* the dork here," Dev said, jerking a thumb in Matt's direction and flashing Amaiya an exaggerated *know what I mean?* look.

Matt and Amaiya rolled their eyes at him and cracked up. They started to walk three across toward the front door.

"How'd you do on that algebra test?" Matt asked her.

She shrugged. "Pretty good. It was hard, though. You?"

Matt knew that "pretty good" for Amaiya was probably an A. She was the smartest kid in their grade. Dev was a close second.

"Not bad," Matt said. "Thanks for helping me study."

"You're welcome." Amaiya grinned, and for a second Matt wasn't entirely sure where he was or what he was doing there.

Ahead of them, kids streamed in through the school's double front doors, some high-fiving, some only half-awake, others nervously flipping through the pages of a textbook before class. Girls gathered in small packs, holding their books in front of them and comparing homework notes. Boys ran hands through their bed-head hair and gave each other the nod. Teachers checked their watches and waved the kids through the doors, their faces tense with thoughts of the day ahead.

Matt loved it all.

For the first time in his life, he was at a school that was *his*. It was his because he was staying here, at this middle school, in Silver Valley, Nevada, for—well, maybe for good.

As the child of two military parents, Matt had never stayed in one place for long. He had lived in nine states in his twelve years. But this time, his parents had promised they would do everything they could to stay here.

And now that Matt had a real home, he could keep his friends Dev and Amaiya. Matt had made tons of friends before, of course, in lots of places. But after a few times saying good-bye, promising to text, and waving as the moving truck pulled out . . . again . . . he'd stopped getting too attached.

But something felt different with Dev and Amaiya. There was something about their friendship that felt easy, as if they'd known each other for a lot longer than a few months.

Matt couldn't really put his finger on it. Maybe it was what they'd gone through together in the flood, or maybe it was all the time since then they'd spent exploring in the Nevada wilderness. Matt had grown up camping and hiking and kayaking and fishing— thanks mostly to his dad—but Dev and Amaiya took the outdoorsy thing to a whole new level.

Before he moved to Nevada, Matt had never met anyone who loved being in the wild as much as he did.

Now he had not one but *two* friends who were even more into it than he was. Dev and Amaiya loved to camp. They were insane and fearless rock climbers, and they could hike for hours at a stretch. They had taught Matt how to climb, and he had taken them kayaking and fishing.

When Matt hauled a kayak behind his bike, with Dev and Amaiya riding alongside and Scout running ahead of them, leading the way to the Truckee River, Matt sometimes wondered if any of this could be real. Part of him kept waiting for the other shoe to drop—like maybe he was just imagining that these were the best friends he'd ever had.

"Listen up, Matt," Dev said as they neared the school steps. "You better not be busy this weekend. Amaiya and I have epic plans. Curtis is coming too."

Matt tried to remember what day it was—Wednesday, he was pretty sure—and what he had to do that weekend.

"Why?" he asked.

"Because . . ." Dev grinned like he was guarding a big secret. "We are going on the most awesome hike and you have to be there. Are you ready?"

"You'd better be ready," Amaiya joined in.

"I'm ready," Matt said.

Dev's eyes were lit up with anticipation, like he was presenting a huge scientific breakthrough. The first bell rang, and Matt gestured at him to hurry up.

"We are going to hike"—Dev paused for dramatic effect—"Mount Kit." Dev threw his hands up in the air and held them over his head in a victory pose. He was tall and lanky and prone to making big, exaggerated gestures.

"No way!" Matt gasped. Mount Kit was the highest and hardest peak in their part of the state. It was legendary for having the most insane views from the top, but also for being extremely steep—and incredibly challenging. Matt couldn't tell if he was more nervous or excited at the thought of climbing it. "For real? I mean, isn't that hike, like, ten thousand feet?"

Even for skilled hikers like Dev and Amaiya, that was a big climb.

Dev nodded, his eyes wide. "I don't want to brag, but I'm basically the king of that mountain."

"Then good thing you're definitely not bragging." Amaiya groaned.

"I've done that hike a hundred times with my mom and sister," Dev went on, ignoring her. "It's hard but it's totally worth it." He started talking even faster. "The last push is practically vertical, so you have to lean all the way forward when you walk." He demonstrated by bending forward ninety degrees.

Matt and Amaiya exchanged an amused look, and Matt noticed that her nose wrinkled up a little when she smiled.

"And there's a climbing spot that practically nobody knows about," Dev went on. "It's off the trail—you have to bushwhack to get there, but it has the sweetest routes. First you have to hike up the southern face; then when you're almost at the top, you stop at this ridiculously beautiful waterfall for lunch. It's so high up, you can actually see Lake Tahoe from there. Then you keep going and you see this huge overhang." He held his hands as far apart as he could. "That's when you start off-roading under the overhang"—he waved his arms in a half circle—"and aroooouuuund the mountain. It's hairy for a little while. But then there's this pristine rock face . . ." Dev trailed off and closed his eyes, a half smile on his lips, as if he were tasting something delicious.

His enthusiasm was catching. "When do we leave?" Matt asked with a laugh.

"Early on Saturday," Amaiya said.

"Be at my house by eight A.M.," Dev said. "Because if you're la—"

Before Dev could finish, Matt smacked his forehead with his hand. "Ah, man," he grumbled. "I promised my mom I'd help her replant the garden this weekend."

"Dude." Dev shot him a pitying look. "That is the lamest thing I've ever heard. We live in a desert."

"Could you help her next week instead?" Amaiya offered.

It was his mom's first weekend off in a month. Matt couldn't possibly back out of it. He shook his head. "I promised. And there's a lot to do—we're starting after school on Friday and it's going to take all weekend."

Matt's family was still living in a house on the National Guard base. They had planned to find their own home, but the flood had messed that up. Their current house had been filled with water almost to the second floor, but it had been repaired quickly. Matt knew it sometimes helped to have a mom who was the boss.

Their yard, though, was still a muddy mess. Now that it was May, he and his mom and sister had planned to spend the weekend filling in the dirt, mulching, and planting shrubs and flowers.

"That sucks!" Dev threw his hands up.

"I know. Sorry, guys," Matt said. There was nothing he could do about it.

"Matt! Amaiya! Dev! Let's move it!" a grown-up yelled from the front steps. Matt looked up and saw that they were the last three students standing outside the school. The principal was waving them in. "Second bell's about to ring!"

The three friends scurried toward the door.

"Oh, Matt," Dev said as they ran. "One small favor: Don't say anything to anyone about Mount Kit. And by anyone I mostly mean your mom."

"Yeah, Matt—it's kind of top secret," Amaiya added.

Matt didn't get it. "Wait—what? Why?"

They took the stairs two at a time.

"It's not exactly something our parents would give us permission to do unsupervised," Dev said under his breath.

"But . . . I thought you said it was safe?" Matt replied.

"It is!" Dev looked at him sideways. "Just swear you won't say anything, okay?"

"Wait, if it's safe, then why can't you tell your parents?"

"Please, Matt?" Amaiya was on his other side. "We just don't want them to worry."

Matt opened his mouth, then shut it. He thought for a second. "Sure, of course," he finally said. But he wasn't so sure. If Mount Kit was safe to climb, then why wouldn't they just tell their parents they were going? Something didn't add up, and he couldn't deny a slight wriggling feeling in his gut.

"We're telling our parents we're having a campout in Curtis's backyard," Dev said. "And Curtis is telling his parents he's camping out at my house." They reached the top step, where the principal checked her watch and shook her head at them. "Hi, Principal Fagan!" Dev said cheerily. "Beautiful day, isn't it?"

"In," was all she said in response, pointing down the hall.

Dev scooted past her and turned to look at Matt. "Curtis's," he said.

Matt sighed. "Curtis's," he repeated. "Got it."

3

SPLAT.

The mud flew out from under Scout's front paws, splattering his belly, back legs, and Matt, who knelt down in the dirt right behind him.

"Scout!" Matt covered his face with his arm. "Cut it out!"

Matt's mom grinned in his direction. "That's what happens when you sit behind a dog playing in the mud."

It was Friday afternoon. Matt, Bridget, and their mom had been at the yardwork for a couple of hours already, but Scout just kept digging holes and undoing their efforts.

"Good thing you're cute, pal." Matt gave Scout a scratch by his tail and gently nudged the dog a little farther away. "But go be cute over there, would you please?"

Matt was crouched down in the fresh soil with a spade in his hand. He exhaled and sat back on his heels for a second, wiped his forehead on his sleeve, and looked around the yard. It had been a hot, sunny day, but a soft breeze was starting to cool things down. The scent of wet dirt and blooming plants filled the air.

Matt's mom was relaxed and, for once, not in uniform or staring at her phone. They had made great progress despite Scout's attempts to mess it all up.

Even Bridget was having fun and not giving Matt a hard time.

So what was Matt's problem?

Why wasn't he enjoying himself?

Mount Kit.

Mount Kit was his problem.

The only thing was, Matt wasn't sure if he was unhappy because he couldn't go, because his friends were going, or because he'd been asked to lie about it. Or maybe, if he was being honest with himself, it was because of all the above.

Scout sniffed his way back toward Matt. He got two feet away and, without any warning, shook his whole body, flinging the mud off his fur and right onto Matt.

"Ugh, Scout! What'd you do that for?" Matt said with a laugh. He wiped the mud from his face and held out a soil-covered hand to the dog. "Well, I can't get any muddier, so you may as well come here." Scout loped over, and Matt wrapped an arm around the long-limbed dog, pulling him in for a hug and a scratch on the belly.

Scout snuffled Matt's ear, panting hot breath on his face. Matt rubbed his nose on Scout's snout, and Scout gave him one giant lick from chin to forehead before wandering over to Matt's mom.

Now Matt was covered in mud *and* dog slobber. "Mmmm, delicious," he said.

Matt returned to digging and dropping seedlings into the ground. As he worked, his mind wandered back to his friends. He pictured them going off-trail on a 10,000-foot peak while their parents thought they were at a sleepover.

A weird sensation crept up the back of his neck.

Something wasn't quite right.

Dev said he'd hiked the trail a gazillion times

before. He said it was hard but safe. But he'd also been excited—like it was a really big deal. If it was that big a deal *and* Dev, Amaiya, and Curtis didn't want to tell their parents about it . . . it could only add up to one thing: It had to be dangerous.

And if that was the case, then why were they so determined to ignore the risk and climb Mount Kit— and so ready to lie to their own parents? Matt tried to ignore his next thought, but it hovered around him like an unwelcome guest: Was this a side of his new friends that he hadn't seen before?

If so, Matt didn't really like it.

And if his friends weren't who he thought they were, then he was right back where he started every time he moved to a new place: friendless and alone. What was the point of staying in Silver Valley if he was never going to be able to make—and keep—real friends?

"Let's double-time it, guys," Matt's mom said. Bridget let out an exaggerated sigh as she dragged a massive bag of mulch across the yard.

Matt tried to push Dev, Amaiya, Curtis, and the towering vision of Mount Kit out of his head.

"Let's get this done so I can go pack, people," Bridget said. "I have a plane to catch in the morning."

"Watch out, Washington, D.C.!" Matt teased. "Here comes Silver Valley's Model U.N. team to take the town by storm."

"Hey!" Bridget smacked him on the arm. "Model U.N. is hard work!"

"Oh, Matt, honey," his mom interrupted them, looking at her phone, "can you do me a huge favor?"

Matt squinted at his mom in the low, late-afternoon sunlight. She had a weird look on her face that he couldn't place. She looked like she was . . . trying not to smile? He was confused.

"Sure, Mom. What do you need?"

"Could you go to the garage and get me another bag of soil, please?" She pointed over his shoulder.

With a nod, Matt stood up and wiped the dirt from his hands. He turned and took one step toward the garage, but something in the corner of his eye made him jump.

Matt froze. A thousand thoughts flashed through his mind in a millisecond. There was someone standing in their yard. He hadn't heard anyone come in. Had someone snuck in? *Wait—is that . . . ?* Goosebumps sprouted on Matt's arms and a huge smile broke out on his face.

"No way!" Matt cried.

"Aaaaaaah!" Bridget squealed.

"DAD!" they shouted in unison.

There, standing by the garage, was Matt's dad. He dropped his camo-patterned duffel bag to the ground and opened his arms wide. Matt and Bridget ran to him, and he wrapped them in a gigantic hug.

"What are you doing here?" Matt said into his dad's shirt. "I thought you weren't coming home for a couple more weeks." He breathed in the familiar smell—a mixture of military-issued laundry soap and faraway places. His dad had been deployed for months, but that was nothing new. Matt was used to him being gone. When you grew up with military parents, you accepted that you were going to be separated from them . . . a lot. It was hard, but it was just part of their lives, like his dad's corny jokes or his mom's amazing pancake recipe.

But living with the constant separation meant that this feeling—this incredible joy when their family was complete, even for a moment—*never* got old.

"Early homecoming, Matt-o." His dad squeezed them so hard Matt could barely breathe—but he didn't care. "Couldn't wait any longer to get back to you two."

"We missed you so much, Dad." Bridget's voice was muffled.

Matt's mom joined the hug, and then Matt felt a firm nudging at his left knee. Scout wriggled his way into the center of the group, and with a laugh, everyone made room to let him in. Scout raised himself up on his back legs and planted his front paws on Matt's dad's stomach.

"You must be Scout," Matt's dad said.

"Scout, meet Dad," Matt said.

"So, you're the dog who saved my kids' lives, huh?" Matt's dad ran a hand over Scout's soft head. "Thank you." In response, Scout sniffed his arm from fingertips to elbow and back again. Then—as if he had given Matt's dad the seal of approval—he dropped back onto all fours.

Matt's dad took Matt by the shoulders and held him at arm's length. "Look at you, kiddo." He pressed his lips together and shook his head in amazement.

"Let me guess—I've grown, right?" It was true that Matt was practically up to his dad's shoulders this time.

His dad put a hand on Matt's head and ruffled his dark hair. "I can't wait for you to show me the town, pal," he said.

Matt studied his dad's tan face, which everyone

always told him looked exactly like his own. His dad had bags under his eyes and at least a two-day stubble. His buzz-cut brown hair was dusty. He'd probably been traveling for twenty-four hours straight just to get home. He was clearly exhausted, but that didn't stop Matt from wanting to tell him a dozen things at once.

It was hard to believe that just a minute earlier, Matt had been scooping mulch. Now, all of a sudden, his mind was spinning with plans for all the fishing, camping, and hiking he and his dad were going to do together, just the two of them.

Matt was ready to throw on a pack so they could hit the trail right that moment, but he knew the routine: His dad needed some time and space to settle back into the rhythm of the household. After some deployments, it was a few days. After others, it was a few weeks.

But soon enough, there would be kayaking on the Truckee River. And jumping off the cliff into the watering hole at the ravine. And rock climbing, of course. Maybe even at Howler's Peak, which was the hardest route Matt had ever tried—and finished.

Matt's heart felt like it would burst. Thoughts of his friends on Mount Kit were far from his mind. All he could think about was one thing: His dad was home.

4

SCOUT HUNG HIS HEAD OUT OF the car window, taking in the passing landscape, his mouth wide open. They were on their way to the airport to drop off Bridget.

"Ow! Scout, you're killing me," Matt grunted, trying unsuccessfully to shift the dog's rump off his lap and onto the seat. But Scout was happy right where he was and had no intention of moving.

Matt settled in for the ride.

"Seems like he might have a stubborn streak." Matt's dad eyed them both in the rearview mirror. "At least he fits right into the family."

"They're a perfect team," Bridget said tartly from the front seat, without looking up from her phone.

"Ha," Matt snorted.

It was just the three of them in the car. Matt's mom had stayed home to catch up on some work—and to give Matt and Bridget some one-on-one time with their dad.

"How long will you be in D.C., again, Bridge?" Matt's dad asked. "Sorry, it'll take me a few days to get back in the swing of things."

"It's okay, Dad." She smiled sweetly at him. "I'll be gone for three days. But now I'm bummed I'm leaving."

"I'll be here when you get back." He gave her hand a squeeze.

It didn't even seem real to Matt that his dad was right there, in the driver's seat of his truck, doing normal dad things. That was the other nice part about coming home after a long deployment: Even the most boring tasks, like taking his sister to the airport together, were really fun.

They pulled up to the curb at the terminal. Six kids on Bridget's Model U.N. team clustered together, holding their bags and looking excited. A chaperone stood beside them with a clipboard.

Bridget opened the door, and a blast of hot, dry air

filled the car. The temperature had spiked about ten degrees in the past week. That morning, the sky was a flat gray. There seemed to be a layer of cloud cover keeping the heat in, like a blanket draped over an oven. It was just more strange Nevada weather, which Matt was still getting used to.

"Still not as hot as Afghanistan," Matt's dad said. Matt and Bridget rolled their eyes in unison.

"We know, Dad!"

"Love you, honey," he said. "Text me when you land."

"Love you, Dad. So happy you're back!" Bridget got out and shut the passenger door behind her. Matt and Scout hopped out of the back to help Bridget with her bag. Matt held on to Scout's leash and stood next to his sister.

"Kick some Model U.N. butt," he said. "Or whatever you do."

"I'll try." The smile fell from her face. "Hey, Matt," she said quietly, "you know how it always takes Dad some time to settle back in?"

He nodded.

"I think this time might be harder than usual," she went on. "I overheard him talking to Mom last

27

night. He feels really bad that he wasn't here during the flood."

"But that's not his fault—" Matt started.

"I know. But he's . . . you know . . . *Dad*."

Matt nodded. "Okay. I got you."

"Come on, Bridget!" one of her friends called out. "We have to get through security."

"Coming!" She gave Matt a hug and patted Scout on the head. "Look out for each other, would you? And please—can you two *try* to stay out of trouble?"

"We'll do our best," Matt said, flashing her his biggest smile.

"That is *not* reassuring." Bridget spun on her heel and headed over to her friends. Matt let Scout hop into the back of the truck, then climbed into the front seat.

His dad steered the truck onto the highway and scanned the sprawling, dusty landscape all around them. "It sure is pretty around here."

"Yeah," Matt agreed. He thought the vistas in Silver Valley were like stacked stripes of color—beige and tan dirt on the bottom, green shrubs and grasses next, then rusty brown mountains in the distance. Usually it was all capped off with a brilliant swath of bright blue sky, though today it was gray.

As they drove, Matt studied his dad's profile carefully. He thought about what Bridget had said—that this time something was different. Matt had been missing his dad more than ever during this deployment. He hadn't stopped to think about how hard it might have been for his dad too.

With his eyes still on the road ahead, Matt's dad grinned. "Whatcha thinking about, Matt-o?"

"Oh—uh, nothing. It's really great to have you back, that's all."

"Uh-huh." His dad reached over and lightly punched Matt on the shoulder. "So. Tell me everything."

Matt took a deep breath, and the words started pouring out. "I can't wait to take you out on the Truckee River, Dad. It's so awesome to kayak there. And then we've got to go rock climbing together! I have to show you how I can climb Howler's Peak. Maybe you'll even climb it with me. My friend Dev is amazing—he can totally show you the basics. Then there's the ravine, the place where you can jump from the rocks into the water, but you have to climb up first . . ." The words tripped over one another as Matt went on, blurting out every detail he could about Silver Valley, his school, and his new friends. "Scout can come with us wherever we go. He's really well trained now . . ."

At the sound of his name, Scout woofed excitedly from the back seat.

Matt's dad glanced at the dog in the rearview mirror and laughed. Matt was happy to see the smile lines at the corner of his dad's eyes spread like little sunbursts. Maybe Bridget was wrong about him. Maybe he wasn't upset at all.

Maybe everything was fine.

"Actually we're going to drive right by the ravine." Matt pointed out the window.

"Well, let's go check it out," his dad said, crossing the highway to take the next exit. "Can you get us there?"

"Sure!"

"So, the ravine," his dad said casually. "That the one you fell into the first time you were there?"

Even though it had happened months earlier, Matt felt his cheeks get hot with embarrassment all over again. It was the same day he'd met Dev, Amaiya, and Curtis for the first time. The memory of flying off the rocks and into the water . . . by accident . . . in front of them and a dozen other kids still stung as much as his belly flop.

The thought of his three friends made Matt feel a little weird. He found himself scanning the seemingly endless mountain range in the distance, which spread as far as he could see. Its many peaks jutted into the sky, with one noticeably taller than the rest.

On a hunch, Matt pulled out his phone and opened the map app.

The tallest mountain was just the one he thought it might be: Mount Kit.

He squinted, shielding his eyes against the flat bright light of the cloud cover, as if he would be able to spot the tiny dots of his friends trekking up the side.

The truck hugged a curve that pulled them away from the mountain, and it was gone from Matt's line of vision.

"Ahem." Matt's dad cleared his throat. "You were going to tell me about the ravine?"

"Oh, right!" Matt pushed away thoughts of his friends. "How about I just show you when we get there?"

It was so hot out that it felt like the whole world had slowed down. The heat hung in the air around them, and they were quiet on the half-mile hike to the ravine. Their feet crunched on the pebbly path.

Scout ran ahead of them in his slightly lopsided, jaunty gait, sniffing at the shrubs and grasses lining the way. He was relaxed and happy-go-lucky from snout to tail, like a goofy kid who was having too much fun.

The rocks that studded the land around them looked like giant stone slabs basking in the sun. An animal rustled in the bushes, and Scout dropped into a crouch and froze. One of his ears spun forward, while the other flicked toward the sound. His nose twitched as he waited.

A lizard scuttled across the path. Scout hopped up and stood tall, his head cocked to the side, his ears flopped forward, and his eyebrows furrowed with curiosity. He followed the creature with his eyes. He was about to pounce on the reptile when Matt commanded, "Scout, sit!" Instantaneously, Scout sat. "Stay." Scout didn't budge, even as the lizard scurried right between his front paws and zipped away.

"Wow!" Matt's dad said. "Scout is so well trained. Did you teach him that?"

Matt shrugged. "I mean, he was a great dog already. But maybe I trained him a little once he got here . . ."

His dad raised an eyebrow at him. "I thought so."

Scout whined and looked over his shoulder at them, eager to be released from his stay command.

"Okay, Scout," Matt said. Scout hopped to his feet and started walking again. Matt and his dad followed closely behind.

"Show me what else he can do," his dad said.

"Scout, *stop*." Scout stopped. Matt turned to his dad, then looked down the trail and spotted a boulder about thirty yards ahead. "See that boulder right there—the one with the big bump on it?"

"I see it." His dad gave him a confused look.

"Scout." Scout looked up at him expectantly. Matt raised his hand and pointed toward the boulder. *"Go out."* Scout followed Matt's hand and gaze and walked steadily—purposefully—toward the boulder. He sniffed the air and ground as he moved, taking in the tens of thousands of scents floating around them at that very moment—compared to the handful that Matt and his dad could smell.

Just as Scout was a foot or two away from his destination, Matt whispered to his dad, "Watch this." He turned to Scout again. "Scout, stop!" Scout stopped in front of the boulder, his paw suspended in midair.

"Good job." Scout turned back to look at them, waiting for another command.

Matt's dad whistled long and slow. "That," he said, "was impressive. Scout's so precise."

Matt was starting to get excited. Another idea popped into his head. He snatched the baseball cap off his dad's head. "Watch this!"

"Hey!" Matt's dad laughed. "I need that!"

Matt jogged up the path. He stopped in front of Scout and held the hat under his snout. Scout dug his nose into every inch of it, sniffing and snorting, clearing his nostrils and sniffing some more. It was almost like he was drinking in the scent, absorbing it into his body.

"Ready?" Matt asked. Scout kept his eyes locked on Matt and gave an eager snort. "Okay, buddy. Stay." Matt disappeared around a bend and stuffed the cap under a large round boulder.

Matt came back down the trail and rejoined his dad and his dog. "Scout," he said. Matt held Scout's gaze while the dog began to whimper and swipe at the ground with his left paw. When Scout was practically bursting with anticipation, Matt cried, "Search!"

Scout was off like a shot, gone around the curve before Matt could even blink.

"Man, he's fast," Matt's dad said, staring at the empty spot where Scout had just been standing.

They hustled up the path after Scout. Matt could hear him off in the brush, crunching around on dry leaves and twigs.

Scout jumped out of the shrubs and leaped across the trail in front of them, heading for the other side. He disappeared again. Matt heard the dog moving through the bushes, obsessively searching for the hat—but also, clearly, having the time of his life.

Matt's dad let out an astonished laugh. "He's intense!"

Matt nodded. "Totally."

After another moment, Scout let out one loud, sharp bark from the brush. Matt and his dad followed the sound of Scout's voice and stepped off the trail. The dry undergrowth jabbed at their boots and scratched at their calves. They found Scout sitting proudly and patiently by a large, round rock. His front legs were perfectly aligned and his ears were pricked up. On the ground next to him, tucked halfway under the rock, was the hat.

"Good job, Scout!" Matt knelt down and gave Scout a treat. Scout scarfed it down.

"That was awes—"

Before Matt's dad could finish his sentence, a booming crack filled the air, followed by a bright flash that lit up the clouds and sky from within. Matt jumped. Scout hopped to his feet and barked frantically at the air around them. Matt's dad ducked and reached out an arm to pull Matt close, reflexively protecting his son.

"It's okay, Dad," Matt said, looking at him uncertainly. "It's just dry lightning." He could see his dad's clenched jaw and the pulse pounding in his neck.

His dad released his grip on Matt and exhaled slowly. "That's right. I forgot that happens out here." He laughed, but he wasn't smiling. "Tell me again why that happens?"

Matt had never seen his dad this jumpy before, but he decided it was probably better to ignore it. Maybe Bridget was right—their dad was just having trouble settling back in this time. Maybe it would just take a little longer than usual for things to return to normal.

"Well," Matt said, pointing up at the sky and trying to act like nothing weird had just happened. "We actually just learned this in science. There's moisture in those clouds, but it's dry down here. So we don't see any rain or anything, but the lightning and thunder still happen."

Another resounding crack vibrated the air, and a flash of lightning burned Matt's eyes. He followed the blinding bolt's path to the ground and sucked in his breath when he realized where it had struck: the top of a mountain in the distance.

The mountain that was just north of Mount Kit.

Mount Kit—where Dev, Amaiya, and Curtis were climbing at that very moment.

A plume of black smoke immediately rose from the summit where the lightning had made contact with earth.

There was a fire at the top of the mountain.

"Whoa!" his dad said, sounding calmer this time. "You see that one?"

But Matt's chest had tightened with fear, and he couldn't respond. He watched the smoke dissipate into the sky, thousands of feet above them.

His dad read the worry on his face. "What's wrong, Matt?"

Matt opened his mouth to speak but shut it again. Dev and Amaiya had begged him not to tell anyone where they were really going. He remembered the promise he had made.

The smoke in the air drifted away.

Maybe the danger had passed.

"Nah—it's nothing. The lightning surprised me, that's all." Matt wanted to distract his dad before he asked any more questions. He glanced up the trail and saw the ravine just a hundred feet ahead. "There it is!" Matt said, forcing his voice to sound normal. "Scout—come." Scout scampered over and stuck close to Matt's side, following his command.

"Lead the way." Matt could feel his dad observing him as they walked. His dad had sensed something was wrong, and Matt knew it would be nearly impossible to convince him otherwise.

He was worried he'd already given his friends away.

As they hiked, Matt heard Dev's voice in his head, promising that Mount Kit was safe. He wanted to believe Dev, to think that his friends were not in danger, despite the blaze of lightning and the dark curl of smoke. Matt kept his eyes forward, not letting himself look back at the mountains.

Soon Matt, his dad, and Scout were standing at the base of the ravine, the cool water to their left, the steep boulder just ahead of them rising twenty feet into the sky. It was still early enough in the day that the swimming hole was empty.

"That's high," his dad said, shading his eyes.

"It's even higher when you're at the top, trust me," Matt said, forcing himself to smile. "And let me tell you how much it stings when you land . . ."

5

MATT DREAMED HE WAS RUNNING through the woods with Scout. They were looking for Bridget, but Scout skidded to a halt and started sniffing the air frantically. Matt smelled something too—it was . . . it was . . .

Pancakes?

Matt's eyes popped open. Someone was making pancakes downstairs. The smell had wafted all the way up into his room and beckoned him to the kitchen. He kicked off the covers and reached over the side of the bed, where his hand landed on something warm and fuzzy: Scout. Scout always slept on the floor, just inches from Matt's bed, like a guard dog.

"Morning, Scout," Matt mumbled. Scout raised

his head, looked up at Matt, and dropped his head back onto his paws with a yawn. Matt ran his fingers through the dog's thick fur.

Matt loved waking up to Scout every morning. Technically speaking, Scout wasn't supposed to be living at their house. He was supposed to live at the kennel on base, which was a pretty comfortable setup, with plenty of space to sleep and play, twenty-four-hour veterinary care, and the best K-9 training facility in the country. Every dog in the unit had one handler, and human and canine were totally devoted to each other.

Matt's mom wasn't supposed to be a dog handler. She ran the whole base and was building up the K-9 unit—she didn't really have time to train her own dog.

But that changed after the flood, when Scout was granted special privileges—or, as Matt's mom liked to call it, the *You save my kids, I take you home* exception. Now he was a bona fide member of the Tackett family, who slept in Matt's room and left for work every morning with Matt's mom. As far as Matt could tell, Scout was there to stay.

As Matt lay in bed, enjoying the feeling of a Sunday morning, he heard the ring of his mom's laughter downstairs, followed by the gravelly bass of his dad's voice.

Matt couldn't make out the words, but he could tell his dad was acting out some elaborate, funny story—probably about a prank one of his guys had pulled in Afghanistan.

Matt closed his eyes for a moment and listened to his parents' muffled voices. Birds chirped brightly outside. A truck rumbled past. Scout sighed and snorted as he rolled over and settled back into a comfortable position.

Matt felt like his world was complete. Especially now that there were pancakes involved.

His phone dinged on the bedside table. Matt fumbled for it and saw there was a text from Dev: *Dude! Climbed all day yesterday and came down to the waterfall for a morning swim. Heading back up to climb some more now. So bummed you're not here. It's awesome.*

The phone dinged again, and a video arrived. Matt tapped the arrow to play the video and a shaky, blurry scene unfolded. Dev was jumping up and down, his long arms and legs flying in every direction, while Amaiya and Curtis ran in a circle around him.

The sight of his friends having so much fun sent a pang through Matt's chest. Mount Kit did look pretty incredible.

Maybe it really was worth the risk.

And maybe he had nothing to worry about with Dev and Amaiya.

"Lunatics." Matt laughed. "Where are they?" He played the video again, but this time he focused on the background. He could just make out a clearing with a vertical wall of rocks at the sides and back. And right in the middle of the rock face, a powerful waterfall cascaded straight down, splashing and churning into a wide pool at the bottom.

Matt had to agree with Dev's description—the waterfall was indeed ridiculously beautiful.

Holding the phone over his face—and trying not to drop it on his nose—Matt texted Dev back.

How much farther to the summit? And is Curtis doing cartwheels?

Matt watched the send bar slowly make its away across his screen.

"Matt-o!" his dad called up from downstairs. "Scout!"

Matt forced himself out of bed and stretched his arms over his head. Scout lumbered to his feet too and stretched out his front legs, sticking his rump and tail in the air.

"You hungry, buddy?" Matt gave Scout a morning scratch behind both ears. "Pancake time."

With a wag of his tail, Scout scooted out of the room and bolted down the stairs, beating Matt into the kitchen. By the time Matt sat down at the breakfast table, Scout was already eagerly waiting by the stove, where Matt's dad was flipping pancakes. Matt's mom stood at the sink in her camouflage pants and jacket, reading something on her phone.

"Dogs don't eat pancakes," Matt's dad teased Scout.

"He'll eat anything," Matt said. "And don't be fooled by his perfect-dog act. He's just in it for the goods."

"Oh, I know what Scout's after." His dad laughed. "But I'd give a million pancakes to this guy, after all he's done for this family." He looked down at Scout, who gazed back up at him with a half-expectant, half-desperate look on his face.

"We have a house rule though, right, Mom?" Matt turned to his mom. "Don't feed him table food out of your hand. Put it in his bowl."

"That's right," she said without looking up. "Otherwise you'll have a lifelong beggar on your hands."

"Sorry, Scout." Matt's dad shot an apologetic look at the dog. "You heard them. House rules." He turned from the stove, holding a teetering stack of pancakes on a plate. "Who's ready to eat?" He put the plate down on the table just before the pancakes toppled.

"Wish I could stay," Matt's mom said. "I'm so sorry I can't hang out with my boys today." She stepped over and gave Matt a kiss on the top of his head. "But I have to scoot."

"Wait, what? Why?" Matt asked. "It's Sunday."

"I know, honey," his mom said. "But there's a wildfire in Pine Valley."

Matt's parents helped other people for a living, and emergencies weren't planned—he knew that. But sometimes he just wished they could get through one meal together without someone having to run off to work.

Matt felt his perfect day with his parents slipping away.

"Where's Pine Valley again?" Matt asked, trying to push away his disappointment.

"It's just south of town," his mom said. "The fire's not too bad yet, but it could spread fast. Firefighters are getting it under control, but they need the National

Guard to set up a perimeter and be on hand to help folks evacuate if necessary."

Scout sat down by her feet and looked up at her attentively. His body language had changed, Matt noticed. He wasn't just playful and desperate for food. He was . . . listening to what his handler—Matt's mom—had to say. It was almost like he could tell that she was ready for action, and he wanted to let her know that he was ready too.

Sometimes Matt forgot that Scout wasn't just a family pet. He was a first-class working dog with an important job.

"Sorry, Scout." Matt's mom leaned down to put her face next to his. "I can't take you on this mission." She looked from Matt to his dad. "I'm going to leave Scout with you two, okay?"

"Sure," Matt's dad said. "We'll keep him company. Right, Matt?"

"Yeah, of course," Matt said. "Just curious: Why isn't Scout going with you, Mom?"

"It's not a search-and-rescue situation—yet. It's too dangerous to take the K-9s out if we're not sure what the conditions are." She shook her head. "That fire could change direction at any moment. It all depends on the wind."

"How do they think it started?" Matt asked.

"Dry lightning. It hit the mountain yesterday."

Matt's blood went cold.

"Wait, did you say 'mountain'?" He tried to sound nonchalant. "The fire is on a mountain? Which one?"

His mom looked up from snapping the buckles on her pack. "What's that, honey?"

Matt cleared his throat. "Which mountain is on fire?"

"Oh, it's the peak just north of Mount Kit."

"Okay," Matt managed to squeak out.

His mom stopped getting ready and looked at him for a second. "You all right, Matt? What's up?"

"Huh?" Matt cleared his throat. "Oh, no, I'm fine." He ran a hand through his hair. "That's just kind of close, isn't it?"

Her expression changed to one of concern—it was the same look she always gave him when he said he wasn't feeling well. "Don't worry, okay?" She squeezed his shoulder. "It's not like the flood; we'll be fine here in town."

Matt was happy to let his mom think he was worried about the fire making it into town. It bought him some time to think. He replayed the scary scene he and his dad had witnessed yesterday: the blaze of dry lightning cracking the sky, the bright flash as it lit up the mountaintop, and the cloud of smoke drifting slowly away.

But the smoke stopped, he thought. *There was no fire . . . was there?* A panicky feeling washed over him. Were his friends okay?

As soon as his mom turned her attention back to her gear, Matt closed his eyes and took a slow, deep breath.

"Hey, Matt?"

Matt opened his eyes to find her staring at him.

"You're perfectly safe. I'll be home as soon as possible, okay?"

"Okay," Matt said, forcing a smile.

She heaved her heavy pack onto her shoulder and headed for the door. Scout followed closely behind her.

"Oh, before I forget," his mom said over her shoulder. "Can you guys finish up the yard today? Sorry I can't be here to do it with you."

"No problem, Mom," Matt agreed distractedly. "Love you."

"It'll be done when you get back," his dad said. "Stay safe."

Scout looked up at Colonel Tackett and let out a soft bark. She winked at him and, with that, she headed out, shutting the door firmly behind her.

The room was quiet for a second as both Matt and his dad adjusted to the sudden feeling of emptiness.

"Ready to eat, pal?" Matt's dad stabbed at a pancake with his fork. "Grab the butter and syrup, would you?"

Matt crossed to the fridge, happy to have a second to gather his thoughts before sitting across the table from his dad. Where were Dev, Amaiya, and Curtis right then? The fire was on the ridge next to Mount Kit. Maybe it was far enough away that they'd be safe. Or maybe they'd even gotten off the mountain before the fire started.

No, not half an hour earlier, Dev had texted him the video of the waterfall . . . the waterfall on Mount Kit. Matt pulled his phone from his pocket to check for any more texts. Nothing. And the response he'd tried to send Dev hadn't gone through. Underneath Matt's text, in tiny letters, it said, simply, NOT DELIVERED.

Matt's heart was beating fast. He wasn't worried

anymore about *why* his friends had asked him to lie about where they were. Right now, all he could think about was that they could be in danger. And if that was the case, didn't that mean the whole deal was off?

But what if they didn't agree with him? A promise was a promise . . . right?

He didn't know what to do.

Matt brought the butter and syrup over to the table and sat down. His dad piled a stack of pancakes on Matt's plate, followed by a giant scoop of fruit. "What's the matter, Matt-o? You look a little stressed."

Matt stuffed a forkful of pancakes and blueberries into his mouth. "I'm fine," he mumbled unintelligibly through the food.

"Wildfires are unpredictable," his dad said, "but Mom said we're safe here. She'll tell us if that changes."

Matt chewed, swallowed, and smiled weakly. "Thanks, Dad." He felt terrible, but he wasn't exactly lying, was he? It was more like letting his parents think something that wasn't true.

Usually, Matt could trust his dad with anything, but this time he wasn't so sure.

He ran through different scenarios in his mind.

What if Dev, Amaiya, and Curtis were fine, but

they found out that Matt had told on them. Would they still want to be his friend?

But on the other hand, Matt had information that they didn't have—and he knew they could be in danger. Even his dad said wildfires were unpredictable. If the wind shifted direction or the blaze found new kindling . . . what then?

6

"YIKES." MATT'S DAD SHOOK HIS HEAD. "If I had known the yard needed this much work, I wouldn't have volunteered to help." He let out a deep belly laugh and adjusted his baseball cap.

Scout had climbed a tall pile of dirt with sticks and wood chips jutting out all over. He perched on top like a conquering hero, his head high as he sniffed at the air.

"So what are we doing here?"

"Scout's standing on the mulch," Matt said. "We need to spread it around."

His dad clapped his hands. "Let's get to work,

then." He waved Scout away. The dog hopped off the pile and ran over to a long stick lying by the fence.

Matt pulled his phone from his pocket and checked for any more messages from Dev. Nothing.

"What's on that phone that's more interesting than mulching with your dad?" Matt's dad peered over his shoulder.

Matt quickly jammed his phone into his shorts pocket. "Oh, uh, nothing. I mean, I was just texting my friend Dev. You met him on a video chat, remember?"

"I remember him." Matt's dad squinted at him. "What's up with Dev today?"

"What do you mean?" Matt's guilty conscience was starting to get the best of him. Did his dad sense that something was up? Matt swallowed the lump in his throat.

"I mean, what's up with Dev?"

"Oh, he's good." Matt fumbled for something to say.

Scout wandered over with the stick in his mouth. He plopped down at Matt's feet, put one paw over the stick to hold it in place, and began to gnaw on the other end with great focus. As he chewed, Matt and his dad got to work shoveling dirt.

After a few minutes, Matt paused to check his phone again.

"Dev still good?" his dad asked.

Matt stuffed the phone back in his pocket.

"Yep." Matt smiled uncertainly. Why did he feel like his dad was reading his mind?

They worked in silence for a little longer. Matt's dad looked over at his son.

"On a scale of so-so to excellent, just how good is Dev right now?" his dad asked casually.

"Excellent!" Matt said too loudly.

"I may have been deployed for a long time," his dad replied, "but I still know you, Matt. If something's wrong, you can tell me."

Matt didn't answer. He shoveled. His dad went back to scooping mulch with the trowel and started to whistle.

Matt's guilt was slowly filling up his whole brain, blocking out all other thought. He knew he was keeping a secret that could have serious consequences.

"Uh, Dad?"

His dad kept his eyes on his work. "Yeah, Matt-o?"

"Promise you won't get mad?"

His dad stopped working and looked up at Matt. "I promise I'll do my best."

Matt looked nervously down at the ground, then over his dad's shoulder. The words piled up in his head, ready to spill over. Finally he looked his dad in the eye, and—as hard as it was to get the first sentence out—he began to speak.

"It's Dev and Amaiya and our other friend Curtis— they made me promise not to tell anyone . . ." Matt trailed off.

His dad raised an eyebrow, waiting silently for Matt to go on.

Matt swallowed. "Well, um. They went for a hike up Mount Kit . . ."

"Mount Kit?" His dad thought for a second. "That the one that's—"

"Just south of the wildfire," Matt finished.

"Okay." His dad absorbed the information calmly. "And why didn't they want you to tell anyone where they were?"

Matt looked down at the ground again. "Because Mount Kit is a really hard hike, and they probably shouldn't have been doing it on their own. But they really wanted to go, and Dev said he'd climbed it a hundred times before. They said they could handle it, but . . ."

"But what, Matt? Go on."

"But if they could handle it, then I don't know why they couldn't tell their parents they were going . . . Know what I mean?" Matt didn't tell his dad that he was upset with Dev and Amaiya for putting him in this position—that he'd started to question what kind of friends they were. That was something he still couldn't bring himself to say out loud.

His dad tossed the trowel into the loose soil at their feet. Matt could see the intensity in his bright blue eyes.

"Tell me everything they told you, Matt. Word for word."

Matt took a deep breath and recounted every detail he could remember. He told his dad that Dev, Amaiya, and Curtis were planning to climb the southern face of Mount Kit and head to a hidden climbing spot. He told his dad about the steep hike, the waterfall, the overhang—and how they would need to go off the trail and into the brush. Finally, Matt told him about the text from Dev that morning—and that he'd tried to reply, but his text wasn't going through.

"There's a chance the fire's not even close to them and they're totally fine," Matt went on. "But Mom said it could change direction at any moment. And if it does, they"—Matt faltered—"they won't know it's coming."

"Is that all?" his dad asked. "Is there *anything* else you need to tell me?"

Matt shook his head. He was relieved to have gotten the whole story off his chest—he hadn't fully realized just how hard it was to carry that weight around alone.

But at the same time, hearing the words out loud brought the seriousness of the situation crashing down on him.

Dev, Amaiya, and Curtis were in real danger.

And he should have said something sooner. Didn't every second count?

Matt squirmed, his insides feeling like a gazillion nerve endings tingling all at once. His dad stared up at the sky, his face dead serious. Matt could tell that he was thinking hard and fast, trying to figure out the best way to handle the situation.

After a moment, his dad shook his head and let

out a *tsk*. He kicked at the pile of mulch at their feet, sending a spray of wood chips sailing across the yard. Finally he looked at Matt, and Matt was relieved to see a glimmer of compassion in his dad's stern expression. "There are many parts of this story that we will be discussing further, Matt. But right now, we're going to focus on getting your friends back safely."

"Okay, Dad."

"First things first." Matt's dad pulled out his phone. "You said they were near a waterfall, right?"

Matt nodded. His dad tapped a few things into a map app and studied it carefully, swiping at the screen a couple of times.

"You said they were on the southern face, right?"

"Yes."

"Right now, the fire is on the ridge to their north." His dad's voice had the sharp, firm cadence of a soldier. "Based on what I can tell from the location of the waterfall, they should be fine—"

Matt let out a gasp of relief.

"—if we get to them quickly enough, that is. It's dry up there and they should not be on that mountain alone." His dad looked around at the still-unfinished yard. "This can wait. Let's go get them. Scout too. Suit up, boys."

As his dad's words sank in, Matt was overwhelmed with appreciation—and with adrenaline. They made a great team—Matt, his dad, and Scout—but that wouldn't mean anything if they didn't get to Mount Kit *fast*. If conditions changed on the mountain . . . Matt shuddered at the thought. They had no choice: They had to get there before that happened.

"Scout, come!" Scout zipped to Matt's side, and they ran into the house together. In the mudroom, Matt jammed his feet into his hiking boots, ready to bolt out the door immediately. He frantically laced them up—why weren't his fingers working? As Matt fumbled with the laces, Scout sat down by Matt's knee and looked up at him, waiting for his command.

"You're coming too, buddy," Matt said. "Let's get your vest."

Matt took Scout's official National Guard K-9 unit vest from the coatrack near the front door. His mom always kept it at the ready—she never knew when she and Scout could be called out on a job. Matt slipped it over Scout's head, buckled it snugly under his chest, and stepped back to look at his dog.

Scout sat perfectly still, with his front paws touching and his head held high. It was as if his senses had been cranked up to the highest setting—his ears were cocked, his eyes were bright—even his fur seemed to stand a little taller.

Scout was ready.

Matt's dad stepped into the room, and Matt gestured at Scout. "We're ready, Dad."

His dad held up a hand. "Whoa, Matt. Slow down. We're going to get up there as fast as we can, but we can't just run up the side of a mountain with no supplies. Let's put together a pack. Have a plan, Matt. Always have a plan—"

"So you have something to laugh about when it falls apart," Matt finished. It was one of his dad's many sayings—and one that usually made Matt roll his eyes pretty hard. Matt was more of an *act now, think later* kind of person, but this time, for the first time, he thought he got what his dad meant. Assume things will go wrong, his dad was saying, because when you're prepared, you can handle anything.

Matt scrambled to his feet and looked around the

mudroom for his backpack. "We'll need water and some protein bars. And bear spray. And a flashlight just in case."

His dad nodded. "Good. Grab those Mylar blankets we have in the camping kit, would you? And a lighter or some camping matches. Remember it gets cold up there when the sun goes down."

"Right. I need a sweatshirt. Food and treats for Scout too," Matt said, adding them to his mental list.

"I'll get the walkie-talkies," his dad said.

Matt's dad filled water bottles while Matt stuffed his backpack to the brim. His brain was whirring fast, but he forced himself to slow down, take his time, and check off each item as he went. *Always have a plan.*

Scout jammed his nose into the open backpack, snuffling at its contents. Matt watched him for a second before an idea popped into his head. "Thanks, Scout!" Matt said, running past the dog and up the stairs to his bedroom. He whipped open his closet door and rummaged around on the floor.

There it is!

Matt emerged from the closet with a nylon-strapped climbing harness in his fist. He ran back downstairs to find his dad on the phone with his mom.

"Okay, hon," his dad was saying. "We'll be fine. Copy that. If you don't hear from us by nightfall, send someone in. Love you too." He clicked off the call. "What do you have there?" he asked Matt, pointing to the harness in his hand.

"It's Dev's," Matt said. "I thought we might need it—well, Scout might need it."

Scout's ears pricked up at the sound of his name. Matt's dad looked confused for a second; then he opened his eyes wide with understanding.

"For a scent item?"

"Exactly," Matt said. "For a scent item."

"Great idea." Matt's dad put his hands on his hips and looked from Matt to Scout and back again. "You ready to move out?"

Matt put a hand on Scout's head. Scout leaned into Matt's leg and looked up at him.

"Yeah," Matt said, "we're ready."

7

AS THEY SPED TOWARD MOUNT KIT, Matt ran his eyes over the curves and angles of the mountains in the distance. Their tall faces were spotted with olive green trees, tawny streaks of dirt, and dark strips of shadow. The peaks looked majestic and serene—but Matt had spent enough time in nature to know that even the most beautiful things could turn dangerous in an instant.

In the quiet of the car, Matt felt sure he'd made the right decision to tell his dad about his friends. There was nothing more important than making sure Dev, Amaiya, and Curtis were safe, and he was willing to accept the consequences of his choice.

Still, he couldn't help but wonder if his friends would see it the same way.

"You need to tell their parents, don't you?" Matt asked, though he already knew the answer.

His dad stared out the windshield and let out a long, slow exhale. "Yes, Matt. I do."

Matt swallowed hard. "I understand." He rested his head against the window and let the blur of desert scenery flash by.

"But this isn't about whether or not anyone gets in trouble, buddy. It's about something bigger."

Matt didn't say anything.

"It's about knowing what's right," his dad went on. "But more important, it's about knowing when to *act* on what's right." He glanced over at Matt. "When I'm in combat, it's easy to know that the stakes are really high. But you know better than anyone that the stakes can be pretty high anytime—like today, or the day the flood hit. So the rules apply no matter what the situation."

Matt let his dad's words sink in. Scout sat up in the back seat and stuck his nose out the open window. He panted into the wind, his ears twitching against his head.

"I know it's not easy, Matt. It means you have to

learn to trust your gut in a whole new way. Your mom and I still train every day to hone our instincts." His dad's voice softened. "And a lot of the time, taking action means making an unpopular choice. I know that can be really tough."

Matt considered his dad's words carefully.

"Do you understand?"

Matt lifted his head from the window. "I think so. You're saying that I should have told you sooner. Even if my friends were going to be mad at me."

His dad didn't respond. He didn't need to.

"But what happens after?" Matt asked. "I mean, just because you do the right thing doesn't make people magically *not* pissed at you."

His dad reached over and put a hand on Matt's shoulder. "That's true. And sometimes we just have to live with that."

Matt dropped his head back onto the window. *I don't know,* he thought. *It's easy to live with soldiers being mad at you. But what about your friends—your only friends?*

"Let me ask you this," his dad said, interrupting his thoughts. "Would you rather take the risk that someone will be mad at you in order to save their life? Or would you rather let your worry stop you from even trying?"

It was an easy question to answer. "Take the risk," Matt said.

"Okay. So once you've decided to take the risk, does the guilt that's eating you up serve any purpose?"

Matt shook his head.

"Right. So now you focus on what?"

This was another of his dad's favorite sayings. *Focus on solutions.* "Solutions," Matt said.

"Solutions. Solutions are the best way to make up for something you didn't do right the first time. The best you can do is do your best to fix it."

They were quiet for a moment.

"Dad?" Matt said. "Can I ask you a question?"

"Anything."

"How do you know—I mean—what if you're not sure if someone is really a good friend?"

"That's a tough one, Matt-o." His dad thought for a second. "I think we have to let people show us who they really are. They . . . leave clues, I guess you could say, with the way they act and how they treat us. If you pay attention, you can add it up."

"Okay." It made sense, but Matt wasn't sure how it

worked if lots of little clues said one thing, but one big clue said something else entirely.

"But," his dad added, "that doesn't mean a good friend is a perfect person. We all make mistakes."

Just then, they pulled up to the Mount Kit trailhead. Matt hopped out the second his dad parked on the side of the road, and Scout scrambled out onto the dirt after him. The dog's vest and collar tags gleamed in the late-morning sunlight.

Scout stood calmly, his head held high and his ears perked up. Matt knew he was tuning in to the frequencies of hawks overhead, woodpeckers tapping on trees, lizards under rocks, and dried leaves rustling in the hot breeze. The dog's nose twitched and Matt inhaled deeply, trying to smell what Scout smelled.

There was the usual scent of pine and juniper trees and sagebrush in bloom. But today, their fragrance was tinged with the faint odor of smoke—the distinct woodsy, charred scent of a wildfire. Matt studied the sky above them and ran his eyes up the side of Mount Kit to the rocky summit that loomed over them.

But they had a long way to go before they got there.

Up close, Matt could see that Mount Kit was steep, tangled, tough terrain, studded with trees, spiky shrubs, and tall brush. Jagged boulders of every size punched through the earth at all angles. They ranged from low rocks to small outcroppings to stacks of stones as big as cars, soaring three stories high. It was going to be a long, hard hike.

Orienting himself, Matt turned northward and peered through a stand of juniper trees. Across a narrow valley, a thin plume of smoke rose from the next peak over and twisted into the sky.

The fire.

They needed to get going.

Matt slipped his phone from his pocket and checked it again. Still nothing from Dev or Amaiya.

He texted them both: *Coming to find you. Mountain isn't safe.*

But the message wouldn't go through.

Scout danced around Matt, ready to go. Matt threw his pack on the ground and ripped it open. He yanked Dev's climbing harness out. "Scout, sit."

He held the harness out for Scout. The dog sniffed at it, running his nose up and down the nylon straps, along its buckles and seams.

The dog looked at Matt, an impatient, excited gleam in his eye.

Scout was ready. He was just waiting for Matt's command.

"You ready, Dad?" Matt asked.

"All set."

Matt looked back down at Scout and took a deep breath. He knew that once he gave the command, Scout wouldn't stop until he found what he was looking for. That meant Matt and his dad had to be ready to follow him—and to keep up.

Matt exhaled and shook out his arms. "Scout, search!"

Scout shot off, charging up the trail ahead of them, his nose skimming the ground. Matt and his dad hustled after him.

The trail zigzagged across the mountain. Within minutes, the heat started to bear down on Matt and his dad. Matt wiped his brow and took a sip of his water, then poured some into his hand for Scout, who lapped it up and got right back to leading the way.

As they huffed along, Matt snuck a look at his dad. He saw that his dad's jaw was set, and he was sweeping his eyes across the landscape, from left to right and top to bottom, then back again. His dad was taking in their surroundings, observing and assessing the situation—just like he'd been trained to do.

Matt knew his parents were always on alert—not just when they were working, but also at restaurants, the mall, even kids' birthday parties. It was a skill they would never unlearn, a habit they could never break. And now Matt was starting to understand why—he could see how paying attention helps you find solutions.

Matt made a promise to himself that he would always try to do the same.

Scout's head shot up and he froze mid-step, his left front paw hanging in the air. Matt and his dad stopped too. They watched as Scout's right ear spun forward on his head, while his left ear twitched backward. It was Scout's signature move—what he always did when he sensed something wasn't quite right.

But what was he sensing now?

When the last echo of their footsteps died out, the air was still. Matt's ears tuned into the symphony of tweets and chirps and calls and tiny claws rooting through the dirt. Scout's muscles were flexed, his neck straight and his ears frozen, radar-like, in position. His eyes flicked from one spot to another.

Matt and his dad stood still, waiting. Matt's arms were covered in goose bumps, despite the heat.

But after a moment, Scout seemed to decide that there was no threat. His body language changed entirely—he went from being on guard back to search mode in an instant. Scout dropped his head back to the ground, sniffing for Dev's scent trail and picking up his steady pace again. His tail was up, and he was alert—like a soldier on the battlefield.

Matt breathed out.

"These K-9s never stop amazing me," Matt's dad said as they moved quickly behind Scout. "Their brains are like . . . I don't know, like computers. Their senses are on full blast every second of the day. Whatever you and I are seeing and smelling and hearing, they're constantly picking up a million times more."

"And Scout is one of the best search-and-rescue dogs of all time," Matt said proudly. "If anyone can track Dev, I know it's him."

Scout disappeared around a curve. When Matt and his dad caught up to him, they found him sitting in front of a fork in the trail. *That's weird,* Matt thought. *Is Scout unsure which way to go?*

Matt started to dig Dev's harness out of his pack again, thinking maybe Scout needed a refresher. But as soon as Matt brought it over to him, the dog took off again, bolting up the right fork. He moved so fast he was a whoosh of brown-and-white fur.

Matt had to laugh: Scout had only been waiting for the slow humans bringing up the rear.

Matt was out of breath as he and his dad double-timed it up the rocky path. Scout skimmed his nose along the ground, the edges of the trail, and the rocks that jutted out all around them. He sniffed at the air, the sagebrush, and the twisting tree branches that had dried out and littered the ground. Scout was practically gliding, moving smoothly through the heat.

Seeing Scout from a distance, Matt noticed for the first time how much the dog had changed in the past few months, since he'd arrived in Nevada. Scout was in the same long-legged, muscular body, and he was as quick-footed and precise as always. His prancing stride was still a weird mix of goofy and graceful, and he was still bursting with barely contained enthusiasm. Matt's mom often said that when Scout was working, he had the energy of all the rest of her K-9 unit dogs combined.

But now, as Matt watched Scout effortlessly climb Mount Kit, he saw something else. Scout looked like the same dog, but he was different—he had doubled in strength and determination. Scout was more mature and confident. More powerful.

Fiercer.

Scout zipped out of sight. Matt and his dad trudged along without speaking, the only sound the crunching of their boots on the rough and rocky path. Matt didn't need to see Scout to know that he was totally focused on following Dev's scent. And Scout would let Matt know right away if he found something—or someone. That's what he was trained—and born—to do.

The acrid smell of smoke was growing stronger as they climbed. Matt scanned the hillside around them but saw no signs of fire on Mount Kit. The smoke still seemed to be traveling from the next ridge over on the light, hot breeze.

Matt kept one eye on the direction of the smoke and focused on putting one foot in front of the other. Sweat dripped down his forehead. If they weren't on such an urgent mission, he'd be enjoying the beauty of the mountain that rose up around them. He'd be closing his eyes and breathing in the warm, fragrant air.

But now all he could do was picture his friends

trapped somewhere in the nooks and crags of this rough landscape—and imagine the look on Dev's face when Matt and Scout showed up out of nowhere.

Suddenly, from around the next bend, they heard a sound that made Matt's blood run cold: Scout was barking frantically, aggressively—like a wild animal. It was a sound Matt had never heard before, and one that he hoped never to hear again.

Matt and his dad broke into a sprint and came around the bend to find Scout scuttling sideways, back and forth across the path. He was barking madly, steadily, with his tail between his legs and his eyes locked on something a few yards ahead, in the brush on the side of the mountain.

As Matt followed Scout's gaze, trying to see what he saw, he felt his dad's arm stretching across his chest. His dad was holding him still.

"Don't move," his dad said softly. He scanned the rocks and brush all around them, his eyes and ears taking in and assessing volumes of information. He was in full soldier mode. It occurred to Matt that his dad and Scout both had the same way of instantly snapping into intense focus.

The hair on the back of Matt's neck stood up.

They waited and watched.

Suddenly Scout dropped the front of his body into a low crouch. He bared his teeth and pressed his ears back, flat against his head. A strip of fur along his spine stood up, and a low, angry growl emanated from his throat. The sound was disembodied, like it was coming from somewhere outside of him.

At the same moment, Matt's eyes locked on a dark shape in the foliage as it came into focus: It was a black bear.

8

MATT'S DAD SUCKED IN HIS BREATH. The bear was big—standing on all fours it was taller than Matt, with broad shoulders and a solid, round middle.

Scout's snarl deepened, and all signs of Matt's happy, eager dog were gone.

Scout was shaking with a barely contained rage—the pure instinct of one animal facing another. Only in this case, that other animal was much bigger, and way more dangerous. Still in his crouch, Scout began to step slowly sideways, as if he was about to circle his prey.

The bear followed Scout with its beady black eyes. It was calm but Matt knew that it could spring into violent action in the time it took him to blink. It studied Scout carefully, sizing up the dog as if it was assessing whether Scout was a threat—or maybe its next meal.

Matt scanned the brush around the bear, looking for any cubs. If this was a mother, and she was protecting her babies, she would attack—and stop at nothing to protect them. He didn't see any smaller bears, but that didn't mean they weren't nearby.

Matt's heart was beating so hard he could feel it knocking against his ribs. Blood pounded in his ears, blocking out all other sound. As if he were watching a silent movie, he looked from Scout to the bear and back again. The animals were staring each other down—each daring the other to make a move.

Matt felt as if they were all just standing there, waiting for an overfilled balloon to pop.

"Okay, Matt," his dad said in a calm, clear voice. "You know what to do." As he spoke, he gradually held both arms out to the side and raised them up slowly over his head, then lowered them back down. He repeated the gesture until the bear shifted its cold stare onto him. Matt's dad was trying to make himself seem bigger than he was, and he was using his voice to let the animal know they were human.

"Yeah, Dad," Matt replied in the same soothing voice, though his was a little shaky. The bear's eyes darted toward him, and Matt felt light-headed. He and his dad had spent a lot of time in the woods together, and his dad had been repeating the rules for a bear encounter Matt's entire life. But this was the closest they'd ever come to one, and the first time Matt had ever engaged in a staring contest with an animal five times his size. He swallowed the lump of fear in this throat. "I know what to do. We're going to give it lots of space, and we're going to keep talking."

Matt raised his arms in the air and moved them up and down, just like his dad.

"Good, Matt-o. Stay calm. Don't run—"

"Don't climb any trees."

"Don't yell or make it seem like you're a threat."

"Got it."

"Can you get the bear spray out of your pocket?"

"Yep." Matt kept his right arm in the air and reached for the canister of pepper spray with his left. He was glad they'd remembered to bring it, but using it meant they had to get close enough to the bear for it to work. Matt honestly hoped they didn't have that chance.

"Give it to me."

Matt slowly passed the spray to his dad, who removed the safety clip.

Without warning, the bear opened its massive jaw wide and snapped it shut with a snort. Matt bit his lip hard to prevent even the slightest gasp from escaping.

Scout took one step toward the bear, and his growl grew louder. "Scout!" Matt cried before he could stop himself. He realized in horror that Scout thought the bear was threatening him and his dad—and the dog was prepared to do whatever it took to protect them.

The bear's ears went back on its head, and it let out a loud, angry grunt at Scout.

Dread washed over Matt. If Scout charged at the bear—or acted antagonistic in any way—the bear would attack.

And Scout wouldn't stand a chance.

"Scout," Matt said, steadying his voice as best he could. "Stay." Scout's ears flicked toward the sound of Matt's voice. He looked undecided for a second, but he stayed put.

"Good boy," Matt said, still in the same even voice.

The bear raised a giant paw and took one lumbering step toward them.

Despite Matt's command, Scout couldn't fight his

nature. His fangs bared, he took another step toward the bear, closing the distance between them.

"Calm, Matt," his dad breathed. "Stay calm."

Matt was trying, but he was close to full-on panic. Scout's life was in his hands. Matt had to be the pack leader and give Scout a command firm enough to overcome the dog's most basic instincts, but he had to do it in a voice and tone that didn't alarm the bear.

Could he pull that off?

"He'll listen to you," Matt's dad said, knowing exactly what Matt was struggling with. "You got this."

Matt inhaled sharply through his nose and exhaled slowly through his mouth. His shaking hands had clenched into fists, and his fingernails dug into his palms. He opened and closed his hands a few times, feeling his fingers tingle.

"Scout," Matt said, summoning every bit of self-control to keep his tone strong and even and at just the right frequency. Scout's ears twitched. "Scout," Matt cautioned again, his voice a little steadier this time. The most important thing he could do was *mean* it. Matt needed to let Scout know that no matter the pitch of his voice, he was the boss.

Matt inhaled again, this time deep into his belly.

When he spoke, he projected a firm voice, filled with conviction—but still in the lower register that wouldn't startle the bear. "Scout—*siiit*." Matt drew out the vowel sound and landed hard on the consonant to capture the dog's attention.

It worked. Scout sat.

"Good boy."

Matt and his dad stood side by side, holding their breath. Scout was still shaking and growling softly, his eyes locked on the bear, but he sat in place.

The bear sized them up one last time.

And then, at last, it turned away and ambled off into the brush.

It was gone.

Matt let out a cry of relief. His dad clapped him on the back.

"That was amazing. You did great, Matt."

Matt was shaking now too, and he bent over with his hands on his knees and took a few breaths to calm himself down. Scout remained seated, whining and staring anxiously after the bear.

"Scout's the one who did great," Matt said. "Come here." Scout hopped up and ran to Matt. Matt dropped to his knees and wrapped his arms around

Scout's chest. "Good job, buddy, good job," he said into Scout's soft fur. "I'm so glad you're okay."

After a moment, Matt pulled back and gave Scout a kiss on the muzzle. Scout licked Matt on the cheek.

"You both did great," his dad said.

"Thanks." Matt shrugged.

"Look at me, Matt."

Matt stood up and looked at his dad.

"Seriously, Matt-o. You were very brave. You just saved our lives."

"No—I . . ." Matt was confused. Had he? "I didn't mean to be brave. I mean, I didn't feel . . . I just wanted to save Scout, that's all."

"Take it from me, pal," his dad said. "You and Scout have something really special. Your mom told me, but seeing it in action is different." He shook his head in amazement. "But that's not the only thing that just blew my mind."

He shot Matt a funny look, and Matt thought he saw something shiny in his dad's eye.

"I just saw my son acting like a real soldier. Calm and in control. You knew what you had to do to solve the problem, and you did it." His dad wrapped an arm around his shoulder and pulled him in close. "You're not a little boy anymore, Matt."

A weird feeling began to stir in Matt's chest. It wasn't something he'd felt often before, and it took him a second to recognize the sensation of fullness and strength that made him stand up a tiny bit straighter.

It was pride.

He liked the feeling.

9

THEY WERE GETTING CLOSE TO the top of Mount Kit.

Matt could tell because there was a lot less mountain—and a lot more sky above them. The peak loomed directly over their heads, shooting hundreds of feet into the flat gray sky. If he squinted at the pointy rocks at the apex, Matt felt like he could practically reach out and touch them.

They had been hiking for hours, and they were so high up that Matt felt perched above the clouds. He turned and cast his gaze outward, away from Mount Kit and over the valley below. From his vantage point, he could see for miles.

Even with so much at stake, Matt was struck by

the astounding beauty of his surroundings. For the first time all day, he understood why Dev had been so excited about this hike. Under any other circumstances, Matt would have loved it too.

The trail grew steeper and narrower with every step Matt took, until it was practically a vertical climb. Matt's worry grew with the altitude—there wasn't much farther to go, and if they were almost at the top, then where were his friends? Why hadn't they found them yet?

Matt, his dad, and Scout came around a bend in the path and heard the faint sound of rushing water. Matt followed the sound and Scout followed a scent, and soon they were peeking around a large boulder at an amazing sight: In a clearing just ahead, a powerful cascade of water splashed and tumbled twenty feet down a cliff, ending in a swirling pool ringed with boulders.

It was the waterfall. The same waterfall in the video Dev had sent that morning.

That meant it was the last place they knew Matt's friends had been.

A ray of hope spreading in his chest, Matt ran into the clearing. Scout dashed ahead of him, sniffing at the wet rocks. As Matt got close to the waterfall, a fine mist of water cooled his face and arms, but he barely noticed. He scanned high and low, behind every rock and in every shadow, searching for any sign of his friends. "Dev!" he cried. "Amaiya! Curtis! Where are you?"

The sound of the raging waterfall drowned out Matt's voice.

But it didn't matter, because there was no one there. The beautiful spot was ominously empty.

Matt's dad appeared at his side. "This is where they were this morning?" he asked.

"Yeah," Matt said, his stomach sinking. "But they're not here now." He kicked at a fat boulder along the water's edge and let out a yell of frustration.

"Matt—take it easy," his dad said, his voice kind but firm. "We've come this far. We'll find them."

Matt turned away and buried his face in his hands. He wished he could believe him.

"Stay focused," his dad said. "Don't give in to the feelings."

His dad was right, and Matt knew it.

Matt took a deep breath and, using every ounce of will he had left, pushed away the despair and doubt. He squeezed his eyes shut and shook his head. *Freaking out is not going to help my friends,* Matt told himself. *Finding solutions will.*

Matt raised his head and looked his dad in the eye. "Okay," he said, steadying his voice. "They're not here, and we didn't pass them on their way down as we came up. That means they're still on this mountain somewhere. They have to be above us."

"Good," his dad said. "Now you're thinking clearly."

"We have to find the overhang," Matt went on. "Where Dev said they'd go off the trail to rock climb." He pointed at the summit. "Let's keep moving."

As Matt spoke, Scout zipped past them. Matt watched his dog make a beeline back toward the trail and recognized Scout's purposeful gait.

"I think Scout still has Dev's scent," Matt said. "Go! Follow him."

Matt and his dad took off after Scout as he galloped through the brush. The dog hopped lightly over downed trees and skirted large rocks with ease, but Matt and his dad had to pick their way along more carefully. By the time they made it back to the trail and started to climb again, the late-afternoon sky had begun to darken.

But Matt could tell that it wasn't just because of the time.

The air was growing hazy with smoke.

The hot breeze that had been blowing all day had picked up, warming his skin and carrying with it the increasingly intense, harsh odor of charred wood. Matt's throat itched and his lungs burned like he had breathed in shards of glass. He could taste the smoke as much as smell it.

Matt pulled his T-shirt up over his mouth and nose to filter the air as much as he could. He coughed, feeling like his lungs were squeezing him from the inside out.

Matt watched the smoke as it moved across the sky. He tracked it back to its source and saw that it still seemed to be coming from the mountain to the north—not from the peak of Mount Kit above them.

But it still felt way too close for comfort.

Matt glanced over at his dad and could tell he was thinking the same thing. His dad scanned the sky and checked his watch, then studied the rocky crags that towered over them.

Matt's calves twinged, and he felt blisters forming on his feet. Between his exhaustion, the late hour, the fading light, and the smoke closing in around them, Matt heard the countdown clock ticking loudly in his head.

What if they couldn't find the overhang Dev had described?

But there was one thing that helped him put one foot in front of the other: Scout.

Matt trusted Scout, and Scout was tracking carefully, intently, as if he was still locked on to Dev's scent. He trotted steadily along, his nose skimming the ground and his ears flicking this way and that. His tail stuck straight out behind him, curling up at the tip, like a rocket booster propelling him forward. Every so often, he angled his snout upward and bobbed his head, catching smells floating on the breeze.

"Oof!" Matt tripped over a large loose rock on the path. He caught himself before he hit the ground.

"Watch out, buddy." Matt's dad gestured at the narrow, rock-strewn trail. "It's getting rough up here." He pointed to the edge of the path, where it fell away at a sharp angle down the side of the mountain. "And that is a painful way back to the bottom."

"Got it," Matt said, eyeing the drop-off no more than a yard from where he had just stumbled.

Matt counted the rhythm of their footsteps, using it to pace himself and push upward and onward, always onward. The strengthening wind rushed past his ears, turning into white noise.

They continued on, the trail starting to slope sideways as they went. They fell into single file, with Scout in the lead, then Matt, then his dad bringing up the rear. As the smoke swirled and dusk continued to fall around them, Matt began to feel like they had been dropped on another planet—the peak above them, the rounded boulders and piles of rocks, were like a moonscape or the surface of Mars.

Matt tasted smoke and shut his eyes to stop them from burning. He was starting to get a little delirious, and he shook his head to clear it. Just then, the trail led them around a large boulder, and that's when he saw it, twenty yards ahead, off to their right: the overhang. At first he thought his eyes were playing tricks on him, but as they adjusted to the dimming light, he saw it clearly, unmistakably—a wide, flat expanse of rock that jutted out from the side of the mountain like an awning.

"Dad! There!" He pointed. Excitement replaced Matt's exhaustion and worry.

"That's it, Matt-o! Lead the way—and hustle."

With a new burst of energy in his tired legs, Matt took off running with Scout ahead of him. They hopped off the trail and barreled onto the tough terrain. The land was uneven and steep, dotted with huge boulders and smaller rock piles, spiky shrubs and dried brush as tall as Matt. But Matt didn't feel the scratches and scrapes on his legs, didn't notice the branches whipping him across the cheek. When he stumbled, he caught himself and kept barreling forward.

The last bit of daylight was disappearing fast. There was a flashlight in his pack, but Matt didn't want to stop moving long enough to dig it out.

They had come so far, and they were so close to finding his friends.

Finally.

Matt followed the glow-in-the-dark patches on Scout's vest, which bobbed and bounced as Scout ran and sniffed the ground.

Matt felt a burst of hope. Scout still had Dev's scent.

He pushed himself to run even faster. His dad was close behind him.

They were just steps from the overhang when Matt

heard a loud cry of pain and a sickening crunch echo off the rocks behind him. He spun around just in time to see his dad fall to the ground with a heavy thud.

"Dad!" Matt screamed, racing over to him. Scout passed by in a blur, his legs pumping and his tail flying out behind him. Scout reached Matt's dad first.

Fear and adrenaline spread through Matt's limbs, making his fingertips go numb. His dad lay on his side, with one knee bent—and his foot jammed between two toaster-size rocks.

Matt dropped to his knees. "Dad, are you okay?"

"Yeah," his dad said, wincing in pain. "My foot got stuck, that's all. But I can't get it out."

Scout pawed frantically at the ground near Matt's dad's foot and whined in desperation.

"What is it, buddy?" Matt asked. He pulled his flashlight out of his pack and shined it toward Scout.

In the beam of light, Matt saw that his dad's foot disappeared up to the ankle into the narrow space between the rocks. It was so narrow, in fact, that Matt couldn't believe the wide hiking boot had fit there in the first place—and he could tell that there was no way to get it out easily.

Matt's eyes fell on his dad's ankle, above the boot, and he cringed. It was already purple and blue and swollen to the size of a baseball.

"How bad is it?" his dad asked.

"It's not too bad . . ." Matt figured it was okay to fudge the truth a little in a situation like this.

Scout was going nuts, barking and whimpering. He scratched at the dirt, digging up twigs and flinging pebbles about. A cloud of dust rose up around his face. Every strand of fur on his body stood on end, and his eyes burned with the ferocity of a predator. Every few seconds, Scout stopped clawing and stared at the earth as if it were alive.

A low growl vibrated in his throat. He was acting so strange—almost like he had when they'd seen the bear . . .

Matt and his dad realized what was happening at exactly the same moment.

"It's a snake hole!" Matt's dad cried, pushing himself up on his elbows with a pained grimace. He pulled on his calf, but his foot wouldn't budge. He was stuck.

"Scout, leave it!" Matt commanded. He needed Scout to stop digging before he unearthed a snake— which probably wouldn't be too happy about having its home invaded by a human foot. Scout stopped, but he stayed crouched over the rocks, baring his teeth.

Matt hopped to his feet and looked around frantically for something—anything—he could use to fend off an angry reptile. He snatched up a long, dried branch and raised it in the air over his head.

Matt was ready to fight.

He and his dad exchanged a look. "Can you take your boot off?" Matt asked.

His dad shook his head. "I don't want to expose my foot—the boot will protect me from a bite."

"Then we have to dig out," Matt said. "But once the rocks are loose, you have to get your foot out of there as fast as you can."

His dad nodded. "I'm ready."

Matt took a long, slow breath and steadied himself. He tightened his grip on the stick in one hand and the flashlight in the other. "Okay, Scout—go!" he cried. Scout started digging with renewed vigor. Matt's dad scooped up dirt with his hands.

Together, he and Scout began to widen the space around his injured foot. Soon, the rocks that pinned his leg were slightly loose.

Matt's dad grabbed hold of one of the rocks and began to shimmy it back and forth, slowly prying it out of the ground. Matt waited, his whole body tensed and ready to bring the stick down on any venomous creatures that might emerge from the hole.

Scout kept up his steady, frantic digging.

The rock was moving, ever so slightly.

"You ready, Matt?" his dad asked through gritted teeth.

"Yeah."

"Three." His dad pushed hard at the rock. It was starting to give. "Two." He grunted with exertion. The rock was almost free. "One!" Matt's dad leaned forward, and the rock popped out of the ground with a snap before rolling off to the side.

Matt's dad yanked his foot out of the hole and scooted backward in one smooth motion. Scout leaped out of the way. The dust cleared, and Matt spotted a flicker of slithering movement under the soil.

They heard an unmistakable sound. A large tan-and-gray rattlesnake was coiled in the spot where the rock had just been. Its tail vibrated in the air.

Scout barked wildly at the snake as Matt swung the stick down over his head. But he made contact only with dirt. The snake had unlooped itself and slithered back into its hole without a backward glance.

It was gone.

"Wow," Matt's dad said with a laugh and shake of his head. "Nice work, boys."

Matt threw the stick off to the side and shook out his hands. "You too," he said. "Way to go, Scout."

But Scout wasn't waiting around for a grateful scratch under the collar. He stiffened and raised his head. One ear rotated forward and the other backward, and his brow furrowed deeply as he locked his eyes on something in the distance. His fur stood on end again.

Scout was alert, on guard against a new threat that Matt couldn't hear or see. He stared up at the peak above them.

"What is it, Scout?" With a hard lump in his throat, Matt followed the dog's sight line up, up, up . . . to the very top of Mount Kit.

Matt went cold.

Black smoke twisted into the sky. Red flames danced on the rock.

The peak was on fire.

The fire had jumped the ridge.

10

"WE HAVE TO GET OUT OF HERE!" Matt cried. "Dad, can you get up?"

Matt's dad eyed the black smoke and hot orange flames on the summit, and the reality of their situation crossed his face. He pressed his lips into a grim line and nodded at Matt. "Yes. I'm fine."

He tried to stand up, and it was immediately clear that he was anything but fine. His face was sheet white and filled with pain. "Help me up, would you, Matt-o?"

Matt eased his dad to his feet, as carefully—but quickly—as possible. He wrapped an arm around his dad's waist to steady him. His dad put an arm over Matt's shoulders, and for a terrifying second, he wobbled like a drunken boxer, hanging on to Matt for dear life. Matt wasn't sure if he would topple over with his dad or buckle under his weight, but he somehow managed to keep them both upright.

"Let's do this," his dad said.

Matt couldn't believe his dad's determination. His dad had to be in excruciating pain. He sucked air through his teeth every time he jostled his injured ankle, but he acted like he was taking a Sunday stroll.

Together, they teetered and hopped through the dark, back toward the trail. Scout stuck close to Matt's dad's other side, his head and ears up. He was listening, watching, scenting—protecting them. Every few minutes, Scout ran a few feet ahead, as if he were clearing the path for them, then zipped back over to them.

Matt looked over his shoulder at the fire. "How quickly can a wildfire move?" he asked nervously.

"Depends on the wind and how much there is to burn between here and there." His dad gestured at the dry brush that covered the ground all around them. "My guess is we have an hour, max."

An hour. That wasn't a lot of time—but it was better than nothing.

Matt ran through his options, as few as they were.

If Dev, Amaiya, and Curtis were still somewhere above them, the fire was coming right for them. Matt had to get to them, but there was no way his dad could make the final ascent. Before he could go after his friends, he had to get his dad somewhere safe. But where, exactly, was that?

It was impossible. Matt needed to be everywhere at once. His brain was spinning, and he forced himself to slow it down and think clearly and calmly.

Then he had it: *The waterfall.*

"Just a little farther, Dad."

"Where are we going?" His dad was sweating from exertion and pain. His jaw was clenched and his hands were balled into fists as he willed himself through it.

"Back to the waterfall," Matt said. "You can put your foot in the water to keep the swelling down."

Matt didn't say the real reason out loud. He didn't have to. They both knew that if the fire made it this far down the mountain, the water could protect them from the flames.

The short journey felt like forever, but finally Matt heard the waterfall from around the bend. Sweaty and exhausted, they reached the clearing, and Matt led his dad to a large flat rock that protruded over the water's edge. He helped his dad to the ground. With a grimace, his dad leaned back against another rock, gently slipped off his boot, and dropped his leg into the water. He let out a long, deep sigh. "That feels good."

Matt could tell his dad was trying to hide his pain. He was tough—a lifelong military man—and he didn't slow down easily. His injury had to be pretty intense for him to sit down and stop right at the critical moment of a mission.

Matt stood nearby, unable to calm down enough to sit. He looked up at the burning ridge and had to force himself to stand still when every instinct in his body told him to race up the mountain. *Every second I stay here, safe and sound, is another second my friends are in danger.*

As if he felt the same way, Scout paced restlessly around the clearing, whining and barking up at the fire.

"We'll be safe here for now," his dad said, scanning the sky. He pulled out his phone and shook his head. There was still no service. "Your mom was going to send her people in if she didn't hear from us by nightfall. Her team will be coming soon . . . then they can go find your friends."

Matt looked away. "Okay." His voice was calm, but

inside, he was in turmoil. He felt pinned between two terrible options. He couldn't bear to just sit here doing nothing. He wanted to go after his friends, but if he did, he'd have to leave his dad here alone.

What if the fire came this far before Matt got back? Matt couldn't put his dad in that kind of danger—could he?

He's a soldier. He can handle this. But my friends . . . they need my help.

Matt studied his dad's face. It was pale and clammy. His eyes were squeezed shut and he lay back on the rocks, his injured foot dangling in the water. It was almost as if he had kept himself together just long enough to get to a safe place, and now the real pain was kicking in.

The day had been hot, but now the temperature was starting to drop. Matt shivered in his sweaty T-shirt. He saw that his dad's arms were covered in goose bumps.

Matt dug through his pack and pulled out a flat plastic package that held a Mylar thermal blanket—the kind used by rescue personnel or given out to runners after a marathon. He ripped open the packet, unfurled the metallic sheet, and draped it over his dad's chest.

"Thanks, buddy." His dad pulled it tighter and shivered.

Matt tugged his sweatshirt out too and slipped it on. He looked back at the top of the mountain.

The blaze was growing. Flickering flames spewed waves of black smoke into the air above them.

They stayed quiet for a moment. The only sounds were Scout's whimpers and the churning waterfall behind them. Matt's mind was swimming with thoughts of everything that had gone wrong. They hadn't found his friends. His dad had gotten hurt. He couldn't finish the mission.

Matt shook his head to clear it and tried to focus on what was going *right*.

His dad was comfortable—for now. They were safe—for now. Help was on the way.

He raised his eyes to the glowing red line and tried to picture Dev, Amaiya, and Curtis near it. Had they found a safe place? Were they waiting it out?

Matt could feel his dad's eyes on him.

"Matt-o. Mom's people are coming. I just need you to sit tight and trust me. Your friends are going to be okay."

Matt wished he could believe him.

11

MATT NEEDED TO KEEP HIMSELF OCCUPIED.

"We need a campfire," he said, scouring the area for dry sticks and leaves. He found a spot on the rocks right next to the water where there was no risk of sparks igniting anything else. He placed the kindling down first, then stacked the sticks on top in a pyramid shape, leaving space between them for air to pass through.

Fire needs oxygen, Matt could hear his dad telling him on a dozen camping trips when he was younger. *It can't burn without it.*

Matt took a box of waterproof camping matches from his backpack and held a lit match to the dried leaves at the bottom of his woodpile. They caught immediately, and within minutes they could feel the warmth radiating off the crackling fire.

"Well done," his dad said.

"Hungry?" Matt held out a granola bar from his bag.

"My favorite meal." His dad reached for it and grimaced from pain. "Is there enough for you in there too, kiddo?"

"Plenty." Matt held up three more bars. He sat down close to his dad and leaned back against the rock.

They chewed in silence. Matt poured a baggie of kibble out onto the rocks for Scout, who scarfed it down in a few hungry bites. Then he tipped the water bottle to Scout's mouth, and he gulped the water gratefully.

Matt's dad broke the silence. "I know you want to go get your friends, Matt."

Matt tried to protest. "I could never leave y—"

"It's not your job to worry about me. You know that, right?"

"But, Dad, you're hurt—"

"I am. And I'm also going to be fine. It's a broken ankle at worst."

"But it's all my fault that you got hurt in the first

place," Matt blurted out, before he even realized what he was going to say. "It's my fault that you're even up here on this stupid mountain." Matt choked up as he said the words. "I'm the one who brought us up here."

"*We* came up here together," his dad said firmly. "And besides, it's my job to worry about you—not the other way around."

"You don't have to worry about me," Matt said.

"Oh, Matt-o," his dad replied with a smile and a shake of his head. "That's like asking me not to breathe. I'm your dad. There is nothing more important to me than you and Bridget."

As if to make sure he was included on the list, Scout wandered over and wriggled his way between Matt and his dad. He plopped his head down on Matt's lap, and Matt put an arm around him and pulled him close. Scout's warm, soft fur and familiar—and slightly tangy—breath helped Matt feel calmer.

"I'm just—not here that much," his dad said softly. "I've spent so much of your life away from you."

"It's okay, Dad. You have to do your job. There are a lot of people out there who need your help."

His dad stared up at the smoky sky above them. "I used to worry that I wasn't here to teach you things."

"What kind of things?"

"Well, to be brave, for starters." His dad chuckled. "But clearly you learned that one from your mom."

Matt felt his cheeks get hot.

"I'm real proud of you, Matt."

"Thanks." Matt shrugged. In the quiet that followed, Matt remembered what his sister had said the day before at the airport—a conversation that seemed a hundred years ago now. Was his dad really feeling guilty that he hadn't been there during the flood? "Dad?"

"Yeah, bud?"

"Can I ask you something?"

"Anything."

Matt hesitated, choosing his words carefully. "You know that I was okay—we were okay—during the flood, right?"

His dad didn't say anything.

"You don't have to feel bad that you weren't here. That's what I mean."

"That's not your burden to carry," his dad said heavily. "That's mine. It's my number one job to protect my family."

"But, Dad—" Matt faltered. He remembered the

confident, satisfied feeling he'd had after the bear encounter, the one that had made him straighten up and feel a little taller. "I can take care of myself now."

Matt's dad reached out a hand and wrapped it around his son's shoulders. He squeezed Matt tightly. "I know you can, Matt-o." His dad sighed, long and slow. He made a face like he was struggling with a hard decision. "Please don't make me regret this, son."

"Huh?"

"Go."

"Go?"

"Find your friends."

For a second, Matt wasn't sure he'd heard his dad correctly, and then the words sank in. He hopped to his feet and threw on his pack. Scout scrambled to his feet, his K-9 vest askew and his tail up. He snapped to Matt's side, instantly ready to roll out.

But Matt faltered.

He couldn't do it. He couldn't choose his friends over his family.

"No." Matt started to pull off his pack. "I can't leave you here."

"Yes, you can."

"But, Dad, what if the fire comes? You're hurt."

"Matt, look at me." He sounded like a commanding officer, not a dad. Matt met his eyes. "I'll be fine. I need you to trust me on that, because that's what soldiers do. We trust each other."

Matt knew the look on his dad's face. His mind was made up. His jaw was set, and his gaze was steady. "Got it," Matt said, his heart filling with gratitude.

"But here, take this." His dad rummaged through his own pack and pulled out two small walkie-talkies. He turned them on, and they let out a static-filled squawk. He adjusted the channels and handed one to Matt. "It'll be like I'm right there with you."

Matt nodded.

"We're a team, Matt-o. You're not going up there alone. Call me at the first sign of trouble."

"Sure thing." Matt gripped the walkie-talkie tightly in his hand.

"And your mom will be here soon."

"Okay, Dad."

"Come here."

Matt leaned down, and his dad pulled him into a hug so tight it hurt. But Matt didn't mind.

"I love you, buddy."

"I love you too, Dad," Matt said into his chest.

After a moment, his dad let him go. Matt stood up.

"I'll be right back," Matt said. "I promise." He looked down at his dog and held out Dev's climbing harness for Scout to sniff. When he was done, he looked up at Matt expectantly. "Scout," Matt said firmly, "*search*."

Scout followed his command, and together he and Matt headed off into the dark.

12

AS SOON AS THE SOUND OF the waterfall faded, Matt was flooded with doubt. *This is crazy. We're heading toward a fire instead of away from it.*

The flames a few hundred feet above their heads had grown taller. They lit up the night, reflecting off the sky with an eerie red-and-orange glow.

So far, the fire had stayed on top of the ridge. But Matt knew that at any second, it could spill down their side of the mountain without any warning, incinerating everything—and everyone—in its path.

Matt's throat tightened, as much from fear as from the thickening smoke that coated his nose and mouth and crept into his lungs. He pulled his sweatshirt over his face and forced himself to breathe slowly and steadily. *Stay focused. If you're going to do this, then do it. There's no time to second-guess yourself. This is a problem, and you're finding a solution.*

The walkie-talkie crackled in Matt's back pocket. "Matt?"

The tinny sound of his dad's voice hit Matt like a punch in the gut. He would have given anything to have him by his side right at that moment.

Matt pulled out the device and pushed the button on the side. "Hi, Dad," he said.

"How far are you?"

"Um, about a quarter mile from the top."

"How are things looking?"

"So far so good, I guess." Matt's voice wavered. No sooner had he let go of the button than his dad's voice popped through the speaker again.

"Remember, you can be scared later," his dad said. Matt couldn't help but smile. That was definitely one of his dad's top five favorite sayings.

"Got it."

"Stay focused. Keep your head on a swivel, kiddo."

"I will."

The trail narrowed to just a couple feet across.

Scout ran ahead of Matt, easily tackling the sharp uphill climb. He scented along the ground and in the air. Matt moved at a slow jog and willed his tired legs to move faster.

Matt studied the burning ridge above them. He and Scout had gained elevation, but had the flames moved farther down the slope too? His eyes watered and stung—were they playing tricks on him? Tentacles of smoke wrapped themselves around Matt's arms and legs. He half expected to feel them on his skin.

Suddenly, a canopy of rock emerged from the smoky darkness. Matt's heart picked up speed. He and Scout hopped off the trail and took off into the brush. "We're at the overhang," Matt said breathlessly into the walkie-talkie as he ran.

"Excellent." His dad exhaled with relief. "Is the fire holding steady so far?"

"I think so."

"You know what to do: Get in fast, get out fast."

"Yeah." It sounded so easy when his dad said it.

"You got this, Matt-o."

"Thanks, Dad." He tucked the walkie-talkie into his back pocket and saw that Scout had stopped a few feet from the overhang. Confused, Matt came to a halt next to him. "What is it, buddy? What're you waiting for? Search! Find Dev!"

Scout whimpered and skittered back and forth across Matt's path. He let out one sharp bark—a warning—that hurt Matt's ears in the nighttime quiet.

"Scout!" Matt said, his frustration mounting. "We don't have time for this." Matt whipped Dev's harness out of his backpack again and jammed it under Scout's nose. He sucked in his breath, filling his belly with air—and conviction. "*Search*, Scout," he commanded.

Without waiting for his dog, Matt took off again. Dried twigs snapped under his feet. Matt used his flashlight to see the uneven ground ahead of him.

But Scout wasn't having it.

Scout swept past Matt, spun around and stopped directly in front of him. The dog dropped into a low crouch, his front legs splayed and his eyes locked on Matt.

Scout was blocking his path.

And he was growling.

His dog had turned on him.

"Scout!" Matt snapped. "What the . . . ? What's wrong with you?" Matt couldn't hide his frustration—or his panic—anymore.

He took a step forward, trying to push past Scout.

But Scout jumped up and, frenzied, ran back and forth in front of Matt. He barked angrily.

Matt took another step.

Scout ran at him.

For a split second, Matt's mind went blank. Was his own dog about to attack him? Had the smoke and the altitude made Scout go mad?

Scout's front legs left the ground. His eyes were wild.

Matt reflexively raised an arm to cover his face and prepared himself for the sting of sharp teeth cutting through his skin.

But Scout didn't close his jaws around Matt. Instead, he planted his front legs on Matt's chest and shoved him backward. Matt stumbled but caught himself, turning his body sideways to throw Scout off him. Scout landed on all fours and raised his head to snap at the hem of Matt's shorts. He clamped his teeth around the fabric and tugged, hard.

Scout was dragging Matt away from the overhang. Matt tripped and staggered until he found his balance. Scout released his grip but continued to herd Matt forward, running back and forth behind Matt's legs and urging him along.

Matt jumped as something singed his arm.

"Ow!"

Matt brushed it off quickly. Before he had time to wonder what it was, he felt it again—a hot sensation, this time on his neck. Matt swatted at it and looked up at the sky.

Dozens of tiny bright spots floated down all around them, like fireflies in summer. But these weren't fireflies.

These were embers.

Matt watched in horror as the tiny sparks landed on the ground. His eyes grew wide as one, then two, then a dozen more began to smolder in the underbrush. Matt's head whipped around, back toward the overhang and the spot where Scout had confronted him. The very air was alight, and the ground where they had just been standing was an expanse of orange—a wriggling carpet of heat and fire.

Scout had gotten Matt out of there just in time.

Matt was overwhelmed with gratitude for his dog—and guilt. How had he doubted Scout, even for a second? But there was no time for thanks.

Matt turned on his heel and, moving as one, he and Scout raced back toward the trail. But just before they reached it, Scout skidded to a stop and began barking in a harsh, high-pitched tone. Matt lurched to a halt and followed Scout's gaze.

Up ahead, the ground glowed with embers. Desperate, Matt spun around. In every direction, the earth was coming to life.

They were trapped. And Matt was paralyzed.

Which way should they go? How would they get out of there?

Scout ran in a tight circle. He sniffed at the ground but jerked his head back from the heat. Matt watched him, waiting for some sign of what they should do next. For a second, Scout seemed just as confused as Matt was.

Then, in a flash, Scout rerouted. He shot off across the scalding ground, and Matt followed. Matt felt the heat through the soles of his boots and shuddered at the thought of Scout's paws making direct contact with the embers. But the dog barely seemed to notice.

Scout paused for a millisecond and looked over his shoulder, checking to see if Matt was following him.

"I'm right here. Go, go, go!" Matt said. Scout sped up again and showed no signs of slowing down. He barreled forward, making sure Matt was still behind him.

They ran for several minutes before the ground beneath their feet was dark and cool again. Scout slowed to a stop and paused, panting. His tongue dangled out of his mouth and his head hung down.

Matt stopped next to him, gasping for breath himself. Scout leaned on Matt's leg.

"Thanks for saving me, pal," Matt said. He scratched Scout under the chin. Scout snuffled and snorted and licked Matt's palm.

Matt looked around and realized they were in totally unfamiliar terrain. He pulled out his phone, but there was still no signal. He studied the peak of Mount Kit above them, trying to orient himself, but that wasn't much use.

He had no idea where they were in relation to the overhang or the trail.

Which meant he had no idea where his friends were—or how to get back to his dad.

His dad.

Call me at the first sign of trouble. His dad's words rang in his ears.

Matt reached into his back pocket for the walkie-talkie.

It was gone.

"No!" Matt cried, kicking the ground. "No, no, no, no, no!" Matt buried his face in his hands and shook his head. The walkie-talkie must have fallen out while he was running.

Matt felt queasy. Not only were he and Scout now lost, but his dad would fear that the worst had happened to them.

Matt wanted to be brave, like his dad said he was. He wanted to feel proud, like he knew what the right thing was to do and had the courage to do it. But right now, he just felt confused and stupid and mad at himself for making a bad situation worse.

Scout whimpered and swiped a paw at Matt's knee. Matt took his hands from his face and looked down.

Scout gazed up at him with big, round eyes. His fur was matted and filthy. His ears drooped. But there was something else in his expression too—something he was trying to tell Matt.

"What is it?" Matt stared back at his dog. "I can't help you, Scout. I got us into this mess, but I have no idea how to get us out. I can't even hang on to a stinking walkie-talkie. Don't wait around for me to figure it out."

But Scout just kept staring at him. Matt turned

away, but every time he turned back, Scout was still there, still regarding him with that look.

Slowly, it dawned on Matt what the look in Scout's eye was: It was trust.

Scout was waiting for Matt's command, because Matt was his person—his alpha dog—and he would follow Matt to the ends of the Earth.

Even though Scout was the one who had just saved Matt's life, he still needed Matt.

No, Matt thought. *We need each other.* Matt thought his heart would burst. He smiled weakly at Scout. "Thanks, buddy," he whispered.

Scout snapped his mouth in response, a silent bark to tell Matt to get it together and hurry it along.

Matt was about to respond, but something weird started to happen—his vision got wavy. He blinked, but when he opened his eyes, things were even worse: Scout had started to fade from his vision. Matt couldn't even see the neon patches on the dog's vest.

The sky was still lit up orange and red, but the world within Matt's reach was growing hazy and dark. Matt strained to see—it was like someone had wrapped a blindfold over his face.

Frantic, Matt took a few steps forward, but he nearly

toppled over. Trying to right himself, he lurched a few steps in a different direction. He waved his arms in big swoops but touched nothing. Without his vision, Matt had immediately lost all sense of direction, all awareness of his own body in space. He could have been floating in a mist or suspended in amber, upside down or sideways.

Even worse, Matt had no idea if all this smoke was the result of the wind changing—or if it meant the fire had ignited close by. He waited for the sensation of heat on his skin. None came.

Matt dropped to the ground, where he knew the air would be clearer, and gulped in mouthfuls of oxygen. He lay down on his belly.

But where was Scout?

"Scout!" Matt called out. He heard one quick bark, but it was muted and far away. If Matt couldn't see, then Scout couldn't either.

Matt squeezed his eyes and mouth shut. He pulled his shirt up over his face and held it there. His lungs ached. He tried not to cough, because every time he did, he sucked in more smoke.

"Scout!" Matt called again. The effort triggered a

coughing fit. When he was done, Matt heard his dog whimpering.

"Scout, come!" Matt choked out. "Please. Follow the sound of my voice!"

Scout barked. He was closer.

"Good job, buddy!" Matt encouraged him. "Good. Come on. Come over here. Scout, listen to me. Just a little farther."

Scout's sad whine was just a few feet away.

"I'm right here, Scout. Right here! Come to me."

Matt heard Scout scuttling across the ground. He stretched his hands toward the sound and let out a cry of relief when his fingers brushed against fur.

"Scout! I've got you." Matt got up on his knees and reached out for the dog. He wrapped his arms around Scout and pulled him in close. Scout was shaking from head to tail, and Matt could feel his heart pounding in his chest.

Matt rested his head against Scout's back and listened to the rapid rhythm of his breathing. "I've got you," Matt said, burying his face in Scout's thick coat. "I've got you."

13

MATT LOST ALL SENSE OF TIME as he and Scout huddled together, blind to their surroundings. It was just a few minutes, but it felt like hours. Matt was on high alert, anxiously waiting for the smell of burning wood to grow stronger or for intense heat to reach him.

But suddenly the wind shifted direction and the curtain of smoke began to lift. Matt looked around and saw the boulders and scrub right where they had been before.

He blinked to clear his vision, his eyes watering. He tried to wipe the soot from his mouth, but his sleeve just spread more across his face. Everything smelled of smoke, from the air around him to his hair and clothing. Matt pulled a water bottle out of his pack. He took a swig, rinsing the bitter smoke taste out of his mouth, then held it out to Scout. Scout sucked down water from the bottle gratefully.

Matt stood up, and Scout clambered to his feet. The dog snorted to clear his nose and shook himself out, his ears flapping against the side of his head. They stood side by side, surveying the endless mountainside around them.

They had no way of communicating with his dad, and no way of knowing where they were.

But, Matt realized, he had something even better: Scout.

He pulled Dev's climbing harness from his backpack again and held it out to Scout.

Scout sniffed at it, then sat down.

Matt wasn't sure if Scout would be able to scent after breathing in all that smoke. The pungent smoke had crept into Matt's mouth and nose and left a rancid taste behind. Surely it had done the same to Scout. Would Scout's odor receptors still work, or would they be blocked completely?

There was only one way to find out.

"Scout," Matt said hopefully, "search!"

Scout dropped his head and got to work. He followed his nose in a zigzag pattern, moving out into the brush. He seemed like he had caught a scent, but Matt could tell that something wasn't quite right. Scout was sniffing and scenting like he was trained to do. But he didn't seem . . . confident. He sniffed, then paused, then sniffed again. He walked a few steps in one direction, sniffed, then came back to where he had started.

He was confused.

Scout was a lot of things—silly, smart, goofy, stubborn, distractible—but he was never, ever confused.

"You got this, Scout," Matt said, hoping he sounded more certain than he felt.

Scout plodded ahead, Matt following closely behind him. After a few minutes, Scout began to move faster. Matt felt a glimmer of hope. Scout's head hovered low over the ground, and his whole body was engaged; it was as if every muscle in his body was tracking along with his nose.

And then he stopped again, his furry tail curling over his back. He turned to the left. He turned to the right. He spun around in a circle and walked a few steps back down the trail.

Then he sat down at Matt's feet. He had lost the scent.

Matt's heart sank.

Scout needed help—but Matt had no clue what to do. He'd never heard his mom or her trainers talk about a situation like this one. He had never learned how—or even if—a dog could scent in smoky conditions.

Think.

There had to be a solution—a way to help Scout get back to normal. Matt heard his parents' voices in his head. *When you're in a jam,* they always said, *use what you know and what you have.*

What did Matt know right then?

He knew his throat and nostrils burned. He wished he could plunge his head underwater and wash off the stench and grit from the smoke.

And that's probably just what Scout would want too.

Matt cupped his hand and filled it with water. "Here, Scout," he said.

As Scout began to drink, Matt lifted his hand, forcing Scout's nose into the water. Scout pulled back and snorted out a spray of liquid. Matt filled his hand again and held it out. Scout drank again, and Matt repeated his move, clearing out and soothing Scout's mouth and nasal passages.

When Scout decided he'd had enough of the unwelcome dunking, Matt held him by the collar and, with his wet hand, wiped Scout's muzzle and snout clean.

Matt released him. Looking extremely displeased, Scout shook his head roughly and sneezed several times in a row. He ran a paw over his head, as if he was trying to scratch the inside of his nose.

Matt watched him and waited.

After a minute, Scout seemed to settle down. He got to all fours and wagged his tail, which Matt took as a positive sign that maybe the dog would forgive him one day. Matt scratched him behind the ears. "I promise I'll never do that again."

Scout sneezed one more time in response.

"Let's try this again." Matt held Dev's harness out to Scout.

Scout ran his nose across it, around it, and over it. He sniffed it, then sniffed it again. Then he sat down and looked up at Matt, an eager, excited look in his eye.

Matt had found a solution.

And Scout was ready to go.

14

IT WAS LIKE SOMEONE HAD ATTACHED a rocket to Scout's vest. He shot ahead, moving so fast he was a streak of brown-and-white fur. Matt ran after him as quickly as he could, which, considering the darkness and the fact that Matt was on two legs instead of four, wasn't all that fast.

Scout moved swiftly and evenly, but the terrain was rougher for Matt. The beam from his flashlight bounced off the rocks and trees around them. Every few feet, Matt had to untangle himself from the shrubs and tall grasses that wrapped themselves around his ankles. The land was dotted with heavy boulders, some so close together that Matt had to squeeze between them.

Matt kept an eye on the top of the peak above them. They were moving parallel to it, continuing around the mountain. A steady plume of smoke still rose from the summit, which radiated orange light. But somehow, their luck had held out, and the fire had still not moved down the side of the mountain toward them.

Matt counted that as a not-so-small victory.

Up ahead, Scout barked excitedly and veered sharply to the right. He was heading for something specific.

A moment later, Scout came skidding to a stop and hovered over a crumpled lump on the ground. He sat down and waited for Matt to catch up.

Matt couldn't make out what it was in the darkness. He reached Scout and, his heart in his throat, looked down.

There on the ground, covered in ashes and soot, was a backpack.

Dev's backpack.

Matt recognized it immediately. It was covered in patches from Dev's favorite rock-climbing brands and a key chain of the Nevada state bird—the mountain bluebird.

"Good job, Scout!" Matt hugged his dog. Scout yipped at him once and waited for his next command.

As Matt bent over to pick up the pack, alternating waves of relief and worry washed over him. This was amazing. This was the surest sign they'd had all day that his friends were here. And yet, this was terrifying. Under what circumstances would Dev leave his backpack behind, and had he done it on purpose—or not?

Matt braced himself and unzipped the bag, which was surprisingly light. He dug through it and found an empty water bottle, two protein bar wrappers, and a pair of dirty socks.

He exhaled in relief.

Okay, so if there wasn't anything valuable in the bag, then maybe Dev had left it on purpose. But why? It wasn't because it was too heavy to carry. That was clear. In fact, it seemed like the bag had been emptied on purpose.

Matt squeezed his eyes shut and tried to put himself in Dev's head. Dev was a skilled hiker and climber. He said he'd grown up on this mountain. That meant he knew how to take care of himself—and how to signal for help.

That's it! It's a sign!

Dev had left his backpack behind for someone to find.

And if he left one sign, he'll leave another.

Matt shined his flashlight in a circle, scanning the area for any other indications that Dev and Amaiya and Curtis had passed through here.

He ran the beam over the ground and spotted some trampled brush and broken branches. "There!" Matt cried, pointing. But before the word was out of his mouth, Scout had already taken off in that direction. He had caught a scent.

A few yards farther along, Matt spotted another sign: a stack of branches crisscrossed over one another in a tic-tac-toe pattern.

Dev was leaving a trail.

"Scout," Matt said, holding Dev's backpack out for him to sniff, "keep going! Find them!"

Scout shot off into the distance, with Matt trailing behind. Soon they reached a narrow stream, where Matt slipped and stumbled on the wet rocks as they crossed.

They passed into a small clearing. At the far end, about thirty feet away, was a huge boulder the size of Matt's room. Scout galloped over and sniffed extra carefully at its base. Matt caught up to him. They rounded the giant rock, and on its far side found a small cave with an arched opening as tall as Matt.

Matt and Scout stepped through the archway together.

There, huddled together around a camping lantern, were three familiar figures.

Dev's gangly limbs were pulled in tight, with his arms wrapped around his knees. Amaiya's tearstained face was strained with worry. Curtis's stocky frame was slumped against the rock wall. His usually spiky blond hair was matted to his head.

"Dev!" Matt shouted, his voice bouncing off the hard surfaces all around them. "Amaiya! Curtis!" He was flooded with relief and joy.

For a second, his friends were too startled to react. Then Matt watched as it dawned on them, one by one, that he and Scout were really standing right in front of them, in a cave, at the top of Mount Kit, in the middle of a wildfire.

"Matt?" Dev's jaw dropped open.

"Matt!" Curtis gasped.

Amaiya just opened and closed her mouth a few times, searching for words.

All at once, Dev, Amaiya, and Curtis scrambled to their feet and swarmed Matt. The four friends wrapped one another in a giant hug. Scout jumped up on them with his front paws, breaking up the huddle with a happy bark.

"Hi, Scout," Dev said, scratching the dog's head.

"God, I'm so happy to see you!" Matt said. "Are you guys okay?"

"We're fine," Amaiya responded. "But what are you . . . ? Why are you . . . ? How—"

"What she means is, what are you doing here?" Dev laughed. His voice sounded weird and small, like he was talking through a straw, but Matt chalked it up to the smoke and dry air.

"Matt"—Curtis shook his head in disbelief—"I can't believe you're here."

"I came to get you guys," Matt said simply. "I didn't know how close you were to the wildfire. Or if you even knew there was a fire."

Matt's friends stared at him in awe. Dev's eyes filled with tears. Curtis shook his head and looked away. Amaiya just grinned.

"This," Dev said, his voice full of wonder, "is amazing."

"Did you come up here alone?" Curtis asked. "I mean, you and Scout?"

Matt shook his head. "My dad came too. But he hurt his ankle. He's waiting for us down by the waterfall."

"But how did you find us?" Amaiya asked. "We're not even close to where we camped last night."

Matt jerked a thumb in Scout's direction. "This guy found you."

"Of course he did!" Dev squatted down and lifted up Scout's paw, giving it a high five. Scout licked Dev's face and thumped his tail on the ground.

Matt looked around the small cave. "How did you guys end up in here?"

Their faces grew serious. "We were climbing," Amaiya said, "but then it started, like, raining embers. It was so smoky . . ." She trailed off.

"We just ran." Curtis shuddered at the memory. "And we ended up in here."

"I still can't believe you came to rescue us." Dev threw an arm around Matt's shoulder and pulled him in tight. "You're the most amazing friend I've ever had."

"I just didn't want anything to happen to you," Matt said, swallowing the lump in his throat.

A shadow passed over Dev's face. "Matt, the fire—it's so dangerous up here. And you came up here anyway, just to save us." His voice cracked. "You shouldn't have had to do that. This is all my fault."

"Dev, no—"

"It is, Matt. I should never have asked you to lie for us. That wasn't cool. And I'm just—I'm really sorry." Dev broke out in a series of harsh coughs.

"I'm sorry too, Matt," Amaiya said. "I'll never do that to you again."

"Me three," Curtis piped in.

As Matt studied their exhausted, scared faces, any doubts he'd had about them—and their friendship—were washed away.

Earlier that day, his dad had said that people would show you who they are—and they will also make mistakes. Well, these friends—his *best* friends—had shown him that they were kind, and fun, and brave, and honest . . . and capable of mistakes, just like Matt was.

Matt had to laugh. That description also fit someone else he knew: Scout.

Once and for all, Matt knew that this time was different. These friends were different. This dog was different.

He would do anything for them.

Even climb a mountain.

A flutter of movement outside the opening of the cave caught Matt's eye. He stuck his head out. Dev joined him, and a look of horror crossed his face—the same terror that Matt felt.

Embers and ash were falling from the sky.

"We really need to get off this mountain," Matt said. "Now."

15

THEY STOOD CLUSTERED TOGETHER just inside the mouth of the cave, gathering their courage. Matt had no idea what they were heading into. But he did know one thing: They couldn't stay where they were. If the fire came their way, they'd be trapped in the cave with no escape.

Scout was at Matt's knee, his head tucked under Matt's palm. He looked up, ready for a command. Matt ran his fingers through the soft fur behind Scout's ears.

Matt turned to Dev and Amaiya. "What do you think? What's the fastest way down? Should we find the trail?"

Amaiya shook her head. "The trail on the southern face is too far away."

"Agreed," Dev started to say before he broke out into a flurry of dry coughs. He paused to take a couple of breaths. "We shouldn't waste time trying to get to it. We'll just have to head down any way we can."

"Are you okay?" Matt asked.

Before he could answer, Dev coughed again, this time so intensely that he doubled over.

While Dev caught his breath, Matt turned to Amaiya and Curtis. "What's wrong with him?" he asked quietly.

"He said it's his asthma," Amaiya replied. "And he doesn't have an inhaler. He said he hasn't needed one in years, so he never carries it anymore."

A terrible feeling washed over Matt. This wasn't good.

Dev's coughing slowed. "Let's get going," he said to the group, wheezing slightly. Scout sniffed at him, his ears perked up with worry.

Matt eyed his friend. By the light of the lantern, he noticed that there were dark circles under Dev's red-rimmed eyes. His face was pale. He didn't look like he was in any shape to make his way down a mountain through serious smoke conditions—with a fire on their tail. "We don't have to, Dev." Matt looked at Amaiya and Curtis, who nodded in agreement.

"We can stay here and wait it out," Curtis said.

"That fire is way too close," Dev said firmly. "And you guys are *not* staying up here because of me. Let's go."

Matt knew Dev was right. He nodded at Curtis and Amaiya in tacit agreement.

They were silent for a moment, watching the sky rain a thousand tiny sparks, any one of which could light the mountain around them on fire.

"Those are going to hurt." Dev sighed, looking up at the flickers of red-hot light.

"They are," Matt agreed. "But we don't have much choice."

"I know how to make them hurt less!" Curtis said. "We have to pour water on ourselves." He pointed up at the sky. "So we don't get burned."

"Great idea." Amaiya took out her water bottle and doused herself. Curtis did the same. "Wet your T-shirt too, and hold it over your mouth," she added. "It's easier to breathe that way."

Matt reached for his bottle and started pouring

water on himself, then Scout—and that's when it hit him. Dev's eyes popped open wide at exactly the same moment.

"The stream!" Matt and Dev said together.

"It's safer to be near water—" Dev said.

"And my dad is at the waterfall. Maybe the stream feeds into it," Matt cut in.

"It does!" Dev said. "And it should be that way." He pointed to their left.

"We passed it on the way here!" Matt said.

The kids exchanged glances.

They had a plan. This was it.

"Let's do it." Matt held his arm straight out in front of him, his hand closed in a fist. Amaiya did the same, pressing her knuckles to his. Curtis held out his hand too, then Dev last. They stayed like that for a moment, their fists locked together. Scout sat up on his hind legs and put a paw on top of their hands, and they burst out laughing.

"Attaboy, Scout," Matt said. "All in!"

"Let's go, go, go," Dev said.

They stepped out of the cave, flashlights on, and Matt instantly felt the light tickle of ash landing on his skin.

Scout took the lead, and the kids followed him in silence, holding their soaked T-shirts over their faces. They moved swiftly toward the stream. The air was thick with smoke, and the ground around them was speckled with shining embers. So far nothing seemed to be catching.

Matt just hoped it would stay that way.

"Youch." Curtis swatted at a spark on his arm. Drenching themselves in water had helped—mostly.

"Oof." Dev rubbed at an ember in his wet hair. He coughed painfully. Matt shot him a sideways glance. He could hear the sound of Dev's strained breathing, even from a few feet away.

"Dev," Matt said.

Dev looked up at him. He looked miserable. His eyes were glassy and irritated from the smoke. His chest rose and fell quickly. "I'm fine," he said, preempting Matt's question.

"Okay." Matt nodded. "We're going to get out of here, I promise."

Dev shot him a huge grin that pushed up the corners of his eyes. "Yeah, we are."

They reached the water and ran into it until they

were ankle deep. Without speaking, they fell into single file, heading downstream, and steadily downhill. The kids walked through the middle of the stream, where the rocks were mossy and slick. Scout splashed ahead of them, moving as quickly and smoothly as if he were running on grass. His tail bobbed in the air as he trotted along.

Matt snuck a look over his shoulder at the mountaintop behind them. What he saw made him suck in his breath and sent a shot of fear coursing through his veins.

The fire had crested Mount Kit and was spilling down the side of the mountain.

And it was headed straight for them.

"Guys?" Matt said, trying to keep his voice even. "Guys!"

"What's up?" Dev asked without looking back.

"Uh," Matt said, "run!"

No one asked questions.

They ran.

The kids tripped and stumbled and slipped in the water, but they kept running, without slowing down.

The fire swept down the slope behind them.

Scout was their advance guard. He pumped his legs. With every stride, his front and back legs crossed underneath his chest, then stretched out before and behind him. He looked as if he were flying.

The stream curved and dipped and led them on a winding route. They scrambled over boulders and jumped off rock piles with a splash. They twisted wet ankles and banged wet knees and jammed wet fingers, but they kept running. Matt's calves throbbed, and the straps of his backpack chafed against his shoulders.

And through it all, Dev took small, choked breaths. He coughed. And he let out a sharp whistling sound with every exhale.

But there was no time to stop.

They just had to keep running.

They ran until they reached a downed tree that lay across the streambed. The kids slowed their pace and, their chests heaving and their limbs aching, scrabbled over it. As Matt threw a leg over the dead trunk, he looked over his shoulder and let out a cry of relief.

They had put a safe distance between themselves and the fire—for the moment. There were no flames behind them, no sizzling fire spitting sparks. At least a mile uphill, back the way they had come, a curl of smoke rose above the trees.

But Matt knew they shouldn't get too comfortable. His dad always told him it was a rookie mistake to relax when you thought a mission was going well. *That,* his dad would say, *is when we let our guard down. And that's when the trouble starts. You learn from experience that it's not over until it's really over.*

But still. "Guys!" he gasped. "Take a break."

They slowed to a walk, then to a stop on the stream bank. Curtis bent over, his hands on his knees. Amaiya walked in a slow circle, her hands on her hips. Dev just stood there, his back to the rest of them.

His head was down and his shoulders shook. Something wasn't right.

"Dev!" Matt shouted, running around in front of his friend. Amaiya and Curtis heard the fear in Matt's voice and dashed over.

Dev's face was pinched in concentration, and his chest rose and fell rapidly but unevenly. Matt noticed that with every breath, Dev's neck muscles clenched and unclenched. His face was colorless, and his lips had a strange blue tinge to them. Dev opened his mouth and closed it again, and when he did, Matt thought he heard a squeaking sound coming from his throat.

It was such a weird thing to do. It was almost like . . . like . . . like a fish gulping air.

Dev was gasping for air.

"It's okay, Dev!" Matt said, buying time while his mind raced and panic flooded his brain. He had no idea how to help his friend. What Dev really needed was medicine, fast. But *not* helping wasn't an option, so Matt needed to come up with something quick.

Amaiya and Curtis helped Dev sit down on the ground while Matt ran through a thousand thoughts in a second. He looked at his friend and saw the fear in his eyes.

If I couldn't breathe, Matt thought, *I'd be freaking out. And when you're freaking out, your heart beats faster and you feel like you can't breathe.*

Before Matt could figure out what to say, Amaiya took charge. "Dev!" she commanded. "You cannot panic! Do you hear me?"

Dev nodded.

"That's right," Matt chimed in. "We don't panic. Panic doesn't help."

He put a hand on Dev's shoulder and looked him

squarely in the face. The fear in Dev's eyes was like a blow to the gut, but Matt pushed away the emotions. "We have to get your heart rate down, Dev. Do you trust me, man?"

Dev nodded.

"Then I need you to trust me on this: You're going to be fine. You *will* be able to breathe. You *will* have oxygen. Got it?"

Dev nodded again, and a tiny bit of hope flickered in his eyes. His nostrils flared as he sucked in air.

"So slow it all down, Dev. Go slow. Innnnnnhale. Exxxxxxhale." Matt took a long, slow breath to demonstrate. Dev followed Matt's instructions.

"Good, Dev," Amaiya said in a soothing tone. "Slower. See? Matt's right."

Soon, Dev's face began to relax, and his chest moved at a more normal pace.

He finally spoke. "I'm cool," he said, his voice tight. It looked like it took all his focus to get the words out. "Just smoke. And running. Be fine." No sooner had he said the words than he was wracked by a painful series of coughs that sounded like they were being squeezed out of him. He closed his mouth and tried to suppress them, but they escaped from between his lips.

Dev closed his eyes and focused all his attention on breathing.

Matt and Amaiya stood up just as Curtis let out a loud yelp.

"No way!" he called out in an excited voice. "Look!"

Matt raised his head. The sun had started to come up, and in the pink dawn light, he was surprised to see where they were.

He'd been so focused on Dev that he had totally tuned out the crashing sound of water. And he hadn't realized they were standing on a wide bluff.

Curtis stood at the edge, staring down at something and pointing. Scout stood next to him, his ears angled forward as he looked down too.

Matt and Amaiya ran to Curtis's side.

Matt's field of vision swooped, and his heart leaped in his chest.

They were perched at the top of a tall cliff, where the stream gurgled and tumbled over the edge and became a waterfall. *The* waterfall.

About twenty feet below, a man sat leaning against a rock with his foot resting in the water.

It was Matt's dad.

16

"DAD!" MATT SHOUTED OVER the thundering waterfall.

His dad's head shot up at the sound of Matt's voice. "Matt!" he called back, his face crumpling with emotion at the sight of his son. "Oh, thank God you're safe."

"I lost the walkie-talkie," Matt yelled down. "I'm sorry. Are you okay?" His dad gave him a thumbs-up and slowly, carefully, used a rock for balance and stood up on his good leg.

"Stay there," Matt yelled. "We're coming to you."

"How do we get down?" Curtis asked.

Matt scanned the landscape around them and

surveyed their options. It suddenly felt as if they had come to the end of the world.

The cliff they stood on spread out to their left and their right as far as he could see. It was possible one of those directions would lead them to the trail that would take them to the bottom of the waterfall. But it was also possible either of those directions could lead them directly into the path of the fire. They didn't have time to find out which it would be.

Directly behind them was the wall of flame heading down from the peak—they certainly weren't going back toward it.

And in front of them . . . well, that was a sheer, twenty-foot drop.

But it was also their best option.

Matt and Amaiya exchanged a look. Her eyes fell to her feet, where the earth dropped away beneath them. She seemed to be preparing herself, and Matt knew she understood exactly what they needed to do.

They needed to climb straight down.

Under ideal conditions, this would have been a challenging—but fun—route for Matt and his friends to climb. They were all experienced enough to handle it—Dev in particular. But they'd been awake for almost twenty-four hours, had hiked miles over hard terrain, and were being chased by a wildfire—nowhere near ideal conditions. They were all exhausted and shaky.

On top of that, the rocks were wet and slippery from the waterfall. The smoke made it hard to see in the faint morning light. And Dev could barely breathe. He was too unsteady to make a tough climb like this.

And what about Scout? He would never make it. He would tumble right over the side.

This descent would only be safe if they were clipped in with harnesses and ropes and bolts in the rock, and if there was someone on the ground to help belay them down slowly.

That was it!

Matt quickly searched the area, desperately hoping he'd find exactly what he needed.

A few feet away, set back from the edge, was a large, squat boulder. Matt ran over and leaned into it with his shoulder, pushing against it with all his weight. It was as big as a car, and it didn't budge.

Perfect.

Amaiya and Curtis watched him with curious expressions.

"Amaiya," Matt said, "you guys came up to rock climb on Mount Kit, right?"

She nodded. "Why?"

"So you have ropes? And harnesses?"

Her face brightened. She knew where he was going with this. "We do!" She took her pack off her shoulders and rummaged through it. She pulled out a length of thick nylon rope, her climbing harness, and a few carabiners. Curtis did the same, pulling his equipment—and Dev's, which he had been carrying—from his backpack.

They sorted through their gear and came up with a plan while Scout sniffed and pawed at the pile of ropes on the ground. Curtis and Matt knotted several long pieces of rope together while Amaiya held up a harness and turned it around in her hands.

Dev sat in the same spot, his eyes closed and his head back against a rock. Every couple of minutes, a fit of dry, harsh coughs took over his body. Matt could tell he was struggling. Scout wandered over to Dev and lay down at his side, with one paw on his lap, as if he knew Dev needed to be comforted. Dev rested a hand on Scout's neck.

"I think I got it," Amaiya said. She snatched up a pile of carabiners and used them to clip two harnesses together at several points. She held up the contraption she had created. "That should do it. See?"

Matt and Curtis grinned. "Amazing," Matt said.

Amaiya had transformed two people harnesses into one dog harness. Scout would be able to slip his legs through the holes, and they could weave ropes through it and clip the straps around his back. Then they'd be able to lower him down the side of the waterfall to the flat land below.

They looked at each other and, without saying a word, understood that they would have to do the same with Dev.

"Someone has to go down first," Matt said. "To disconnect them when they get to the bottom." He looked from Curtis to Amaiya and back again. "But I need to stay here with Scout. So, which one of you wants to go?"

Matt knew it was a big ask. Whoever went first was the guinea pig who would test whether the system they had rigged would work . . . or not.

Curtis bit his lip and Amaiya swallowed hard.

"I'll do it," they said at the same time. Then they both laughed nervously.

"Amaiya," Curtis said, his tone growing serious, "let me do it. You stay here with Dev. He needs you."

He was right, and Amaiya knew it. She nodded.

They stood up. Curtis stepped into his own harness and clipped himself into one end of the rope. Matt wrapped the other end of the rope around his waist and tied it with a military-grade knot his dad had taught him. Gathering up the rest of the slack, he walked over to the boulder and circled it, then sat down on the ground facing it, with his back to his friends. He stretched out his legs and put the soles of his feet firmly against the rock.

On one end of the rope, Matt would brace himself against the boulder. On the other end, Curtis would lower himself slowly down the side of the cliff. In between them, the rope would wrap around the giant rock, which would serve as a sort of pulley, doing much of the work of supporting Curtis's weight and helping Matt control the rope.

Matt had taken off his sweatshirt, and he used the sleeves as makeshift gloves so the rope wouldn't burn his hands. He looked over at Amaiya and Curtis.

Amaiya was checking Curtis's harness. She stepped back. Curtis gave Matt a thumbs-up, and Matt nodded in return.

They were ready.

17

MATT SUCKED IN HIS BREATH, then let out one long, slow exhale. He shook out his legs and hands and gripped the rope tightly. Then he felt it go taut as Curtis began his descent. Little by little, responding to the tension in the rope, Matt let out the slack, and slowly, Curtis made his way to the ground.

Matt couldn't believe how heavy his friend felt— even with the boulder distributing his weight. Matt's knees locked and his legs twitched. His forearms shook with exertion, and the muscles in his back flexed so tightly it felt like they would snap. The rope threatened to pop out of his hands at any moment. Scout sat next to him, close enough to let Matt know he was there to help, but keeping a watchful eye on the edge of the cliff.

It felt like an eternity. Matt gritted his teeth and wiped the sweat from his brow with his shoulder. He took quick, sharp breaths through his nose. He didn't think about all the ways this jury-rigged system could go terribly wrong, or the fact that a fire could be swooping down on them at any moment, or that he still had to do this twice more—once for Dev and once for Scout—before he could even begin to figure out how to get his dad off the mountain with a busted leg.

Instead, Matt focused on one inch of rope at a time, and then the next inch, then the next. He listened for the sound of Amaiya's voice as she called out the distance Curtis had left to travel. "Ten feet," she said. "Nine. Eight . . ."

Finally, Matt lurched backward as the tension in the rope disappeared. Curtis had his feet on solid ground.

"I got him!" Matt's dad yelled up from below. Matt felt the rope vibrate as his dad untied Curtis from the harness.

Matt's whole body was trembling—as much from the effort as from the nerves.

Their plan had worked.

Matt quickly pulled the rope back up and took a moment to catch his breath. It was Dev's turn. Matt stood up and walked over to his friend, who was breathing more easily but still seemed really out of it. Matt and Amaiya helped Dev stand up and eased the harness around him. Scout circled them, supervising.

Dev would have to hold on to the rope to keep himself upright as Matt lowered him down.

"Dev, you understand what's happening here?" Matt asked.

"I understand," Dev said, his eyelids heavy and his chest letting out strange squeaking sounds with every breath he took. "I get it."

"You're going to be clipped in, but you'll also need to hang on to the rope, okay?"

"Yep. Hang on. Got it."

"Hey, man," Matt said, putting his hands on Dev's shoulders and looking up into his much taller friend's face. "You're going to do great. Curtis and my dad are on the ground waiting for you."

Dev looked Matt right in the eye and grinned. "Neither one of them is soft enough to break my fall, so I plan to hang on tight."

Matt and Amaiya rolled their eyes.

"That's the spirit, Dev," Amaiya teased him.

Matt punched Dev in the shoulder—just like Dev always punched Matt.

Then Matt walked around the boulder and sat down again.

It pained Matt to think of his friend being so helpless, especially on a route he would be excited to tackle under normal circumstances. Dev was an insane rock climber. When he climbed, he was in total control of his body, but at the same time he looked so free, as though he was a part of nature.

But today, Dev's body was working against him. Instead, he would be strapped into a harness, clinging to a rope, while he was lowered slowly to the ground.

It wasn't right. But Matt knew it was their only choice.

"On three," Amaiya called out. Matt was facing away from them, but he could hear her guiding Dev over the side of the mountain. Matt felt the rope go taut, and he began to let out the slack.

Amaiya alternated between encouraging Dev and calling out the remaining distance to Matt. Matt's leg muscles burned, and his back ached. His hands chafed even through the sweatshirt.

"Thirteen. Twelve," Amaiya called out. "Elev—
Dev!" she shrieked.

The rope jerked Matt's arms, hard. "Amaiya!" he
screamed. "What's happening?" Scout hopped to his
feet and ran to Amaiya in a few long strides.

Matt felt as if the weight on the other end of the
rope had suddenly doubled. The rope vibrated and
yanked his arms, making his knees feel like they were
about to buckle under the strain. He pushed even
harder against his feet to keep himself from being
dragged right around the rock. "I can't hold on—"

"It's Dev," she shouted back. "He passed out and
let go of the rope. He's just—he's dangling there. Dev!
Wake up! Wake up!"

Through the sound of the blood pounding in his
ears, Matt heard Scout's familiar whimper and whine.
The dog scampered toward the edge of the cliff.

Matt used every muscle in his body to hold the
rope—and himself—steady. Adrenaline pumped
through him, and he felt dizzy with fear. He shut his
eyes until it passed, but two terrible thoughts played
on repeat in Matt's head: If he couldn't hold on, Dev
would plummet straight down onto a hard stone
surface.

And if that happened, Dev would never survive.

Scout started barking—a loud and relentless barrage of noise that was unlike anything Matt had ever heard. Even without seeing him, Matt knew what Scout was doing. He was trying to wake up Dev.

Suddenly the rope jerked and the weight grew steady again. Scout did it!

Matt heard Dev's faint voice echoing off the rocks. "Sorry," Dev said.

"Are you okay?" Amaiya called down to him.

"Yep. Won't happen again."

"It better not," she said. "Don't you dare scare me like that."

Matt's hands were cramping. He couldn't hold on much longer.

"Enough chatting," he shouted. "Keep it moving, Dev."

"Wow," Dev called up in response. "So impatient."

Matt was happy to hear that his friend—his extremely sarcastic friend—was himself again.

"Five," Amaiya called. "Four . . ." Then, at last, Matt felt the beautiful relief of weightlessness in his arms.

Dev had made it to the bottom.

"Dev's good!" Matt's dad shouted up. "I got him!"

Scout felt light as a feather compared to Dev's deadweight. After the dog was safely on the ground below, Matt and Amaiya threw the rest of the gear over the cliff and climbed down on their own, slowly and carefully.

As soon as Matt's feet touched solid ground, he ran straight to his dad.

So many emotions passed across his dad's face in rapid succession that Matt couldn't track them all. His dad opened and closed his mouth, like he wanted to say something. But instead of speaking, he folded Matt into a hug of near-crushing strength. Matt sank into his dad's arms. Scout hopped up and wormed his way between them, and they stood like that for a long moment.

Matt's dad released him and turned to the other dirt-streaked, ash-covered kids. For an excruciatingly long moment, his face was blank as he studied them one by one. Matt didn't know what he was going to say. Would he scold them for going up Mount Kit without permission in the first place?

And then his dad's face broke into a huge grin. "I am so incredibly glad you're all okay."

"You too, Mr. Tackett," Amaiya said.

"Thank you for coming to rescue us," Curtis said.

But Matt's dad didn't hear them. His attention had been drawn away, and he was focusing intently on something. Matt followed his gaze and saw that he was staring at Dev.

"Dev?" Matt's dad asked, a note of worry in his voice.

Dev's breathing had gotten worse. Matt heard that sound again—a ragged, rapid sucking in of air that made Matt's chest hurt just to listen to it.

"You're wheezing, Dev," Matt's dad said.

Dev nodded. "Yeah," he managed to squeak out.

"When we can calm him down, he can breathe better," Matt told his dad. "And his cough sounds really dry—like he needs steam or something."

"He does," Matt's dad said. "He needs humidity."

Matt eyed the water nearby. "Sit down," he said to Dev.

"Yessir." Dev raised two fingers to his forehead in a mock salute.

"Isn't he hilarious?" Matt said to his dad.

Dev sat, and Scout plopped down next to him.

Matt grabbed a scrap of fabric off the ground left over from a T-shirt his dad had ripped up to make a splint. Matt ran to the stream, then dipped the fabric in the water, squeezed it out, and ran back over to Dev.

Matt gave Dev the wet cloth. "Hold this over your mouth," Matt instructed him. "It'll humidify the air you're breathing in."

"Good thinking, Matt-o," his dad said. He turned to Dev. "Dev, I want you to lean back. That's right—sit up as straight as you can. That'll open up your airways. Breathe in through your nose—count to four. Good. And purse your lips when you exhale, like this." Matt's dad made an O with his lips and blew through them slowly.

Dev nodded and did as he was told.

"Inhale, exhale," Matt said. "That's all you need to think about right now. We're going to take care of the rest. Inhale, exhale."

"No fear, Dev," Matt's dad said. "No fear."

Scout crawled halfway onto Dev's lap, and Dev put his hand on Scout's back. His arm rose and fell with Scout's breathing.

They all watched as Dev began to visibly relax. Dev's chest slowed its frenzied rise and fall, and soon he was breathing in sync with Scout.

"Nice, Dev," Matt exhaled.

Matt's dad clapped him on the shoulder. "We make a pretty good team, Matt-o."

Matt couldn't fight a smile. "We do."

He had pictured his dad doing his job a million times over the years. He had imagined his dad making split-second decisions in pretty rough situations, and now he'd gotten to see him in action. Instead of being paralyzed with fear or scared about his injuries, his dad was so calm, so certain of what to do.

And Matt had been right by his side.

"I know you don't like to take a compliment, Matt-o," his dad said, "but I'm proud of you. You've been very brave up here."

"Yeah, you're really calm under pressure, Matt," Amaiya said.

"Me?" Matt felt his cheeks get hot.

"Yeah, you."

"Don't let it go to your head," Dev called from his spot on the ground.

"It's true," Curtis added. "You always seem to know what to do."

"Oh—uh—I—I don't." He looked at his dad. "But I guess I learned from my parents that you just have to figure it out." Matt's dad beamed at him.

In that moment, more than ever, Matt was proud to be his father's son.

But now everyone was staring at him, and Matt squirmed.

"By the way," his dad said, "you guys really stink. You smell like a barbecue."

18

WITH A FLASH OF SUDDEN MOVEMENT, Scout scrambled to his feet and ran over to Matt. He jumped up and put his front paws smack in the middle of Matt's chest. But he wasn't there to play.

Scout dropped back to the ground and, with his eyes still on Matt, skittered sideways, barking frantically, wildly. He sounded desperate—even scared.

Scout was warning them about something.

His ears were back and his tail pointed straight out behind him. He looked up into the sky. Matt's stomach churned as he turned to look too. He knew what was there before he saw it: the fire.

It had reached them.

Flames licked the cliff at the top of the waterfall, where they had just been. A swirling mass of black smoke unfurled in the sky.

It was only a matter of seconds before the fire jumped the cliff and ignited the land around them.

There was no time to run.

"In the water—now!" Matt's dad shouted. "Everyone—go, go, go!" Matt and Amaiya yanked Dev to his feet, while Curtis steadied Matt's dad. The unwieldy entourage half ran, half stumbled to the pool of water at the bottom of the waterfall. Matt saw that his dad's face was screwed up tightly, his teeth gritted against the pain. He sucked in his breath with every step, but he was focused and determined. Matt forced himself not to think about the serious damage his dad was probably doing to his injured ankle.

They threw themselves into the neck-deep water. Scout landed with a loud splash right next to Matt and started dogpaddling quickly. He tilted his head back to hold his snout above the waterline. His front paws cut through the surface, then disappeared again, over and over.

Nearby, Matt's dad hopped through the water on one foot. Matt's whole body hurt from the shock of the temperature, but he knew it was nowhere near the level of pain his dad had to be feeling—or the anxiety Dev had been fighting off as he tried to breathe.

Matt saw the others glancing up at the sky. He looked up too and watched the air darken into a deep, dull gray. Within seconds it felt dark as night—the very air around them seemed opaque and solid.

Dev began to cough, and then they all did, choking on the smoke. They pulled their wet shirts up over their mouths and noses in a desperate attempt to filter the toxic air. Matt's eyes burned so badly he could barely keep them open.

Off to their right, Matt spotted a horizontal rock jutting out over the water, creating an overhang about six feet wide. There was a foot or so of space between the surface of the water and the rock—just enough for them to keep their heads above water while being protected from above.

"There!" He pointed to the rock, and they all swam toward it. The group huddled together underneath, waiting. Dev struggled to catch his breath, but being in the water seemed to have helped. At least he wasn't gasping for oxygen like before.

No sooner did they take shelter under the rock than

a barrage of fireballs fell from the sky. But it wasn't just embers anymore—now it was fiery pieces of tree bark and blazing clusters of leaves. The smoke grew so thick that Matt couldn't see more than a couple of feet in front of him.

He feared the worst. He looked around and saw that they all did. Even his dad.

After everything they had been through on Mount Kit, was this it? Was this as far as they could go? As close as they were going to get to safety?

With every passing second, the air grew hotter, but Matt was shivering from the cold water and the shock of their situation. No one spoke—no one *could* speak.

Matt felt like they would run out of air at any second. But he also knew that when the fire dropped over the cliff toward them, they'd have to dive under the water to protect themselves from the flames. Either way, he wasn't sure how they would breathe.

It was bad. Very, very bad.

Matt reached out a hand to his dad. His dad grabbed it and gave it a squeeze.

"When the fire gets here," Matt said to the group, "go under."

"Okay," Curtis replied, his voice tense.

"Got it." Amaiya was resolute.

"Dev, you got this?" Matt asked.

"Definitely," Dev rasped.

Matt peeked out from under the rock. The dark sky was infused with an orange glow, which spread all around them and lit up the gray dome of smoke. Matt's face grew hot as a deafening roar blasted his ears—it was as loud as a military jet landing.

The fire was there.

"Underwater!" Matt shouted. "Now!"

Five people ducked their heads below the surface. Matt pulled Scout down with him.

Matt clamped his mouth shut and held on to his dog for dear life.

19

MATT THOUGHT HIS LUNGS WOULD BURST. His head exploded with a thousand tiny pinpoints of light and sound. Scout struggled in his arms.

Finally Matt couldn't bear the pressure in his chest for another second. He thrust his head above the surface of the water, pulling Scout up with him. A wall of heat slammed into them.

It wasn't safe to stay above the water.

Scout and Matt sucked in huge mouthfuls of smoky air. As soon as Matt's vision cleared, he took in the terrifying sight that surrounded them on all sides.

Everything was on fire.

Underbrush and trees, shrubs and grasses. Twigs

and fallen tree limbs. Everything burned hot and red and angry.

One by one, the others came up for air too.

"Everyone okay?" Matt's dad gasped. Amaiya and Curtis nodded, their chests heaving. "Good. Get back under." The three of them submerged themselves again.

But Dev just stood there, looking dazed. Even from a few feet away, Matt could see his nostrils flaring. He exhaled in ragged spurts. "Dev?" Matt cried.

Dev didn't respond. It was as if he were in a faraway place, unable to even hear the sound of Matt's voice. *"Dev!"* Matt shouted.

Dev just stared into the distance.

Matt desperately needed to shake his friend back to reality. But before Matt could reach him, Dev's eyes began to droop, then slowly close. He watched in horror as Dev passed out and slipped down into the water.

The top of Dev's head disappeared with a soft *plink*.

"No!" Matt screamed, releasing Scout. "No, no, no, no, no—Dev!" Matt kicked off the ground with one foot and started to swim toward Dev. But Scout pushed past him, leaving Matt in his wake. Scout paddled hard and fast, and before Matt could even call Scout's name, the dog was underwater, diving toward the spot where Dev had disappeared.

Matt couldn't bear the sensation that overcame him. It wasn't fear, and it wasn't despair. It wasn't panic, and it wasn't a frustrated desire to turn back time, even by a few seconds. It was all of these emotions combined— and then some.

Now his best friend and Scout were *both* gone.

Matt swam toward them just as the others rose to the surface to take another gulp of air.

"Matt!" his dad said, alarmed. "What are you doing?! Get back under—" But when his dad saw the look on Matt's face, he instantly understood.

Matt and his dad reached the spot where Dev and Scout had gone under. They both took huge swallows of air and dove below the debris-covered surface. It was impossible to see in the dark water. Diving toward the bottom of the pond, Matt waved his arms around wildly, desperate to make contact.

Nothing.

Matt needed air badly. He broke the surface and saw his dad standing, holding Dev under the armpits while Dev coughed up water.

"I'm okay," Dev said weakly.

Matt spun around in a circle, frantically searching for Scout. But he wasn't there. "Scout?" Matt called. "Scout! Buddy! Where are you?" Matt's movements sent ripples out across the surface of the water. "Scout!"

"There!" his dad shouted.

Matt turned, and there, about five feet away, floating out from under the protection of the rock, was Scout. His head bobbed on the water. His eyes were open, but he was listless and only semiconscious. Scout paddled feebly a couple of times, trying his best to stay afloat.

Matt's heart stopped in his chest. The air was searing hot, but he didn't care. He swam to Scout and, in an instant, scooped him up and dragged him back toward the overhang, paddling with one arm. Scout hung like a ragdoll, not moving or responding to Matt's touch.

The other kids looked on in horror, their eyes wide and brimming with tears. Curtis held a hand over his mouth, and Amaiya looked away, blinking.

"Dad!" Matt cried. "Dad, is he okay? What's wrong with him?"

"I—I don't know, Matt," his dad said softly. "But we're going to take care of him."

As if from a great distance, Matt heard a steady churning sound echoing off the rocks. He was too focused on Scout to care that the sound drew closer, growing so loud it thunked like a drum in his chest. He barely noticed when a deluge of water rained down from the sky, dumped from two large aircraft passing overhead.

Helicopters.

Water helicopters.

They had come to put out the wildfire.

The aircraft flew on, leaving a doused, steaming landscape behind them. Matt lugged his limp, wet dog up onto the bank and laid Scout down on the rocks. All around them, charred trees and brush smoldered. The others climbed out of the water too. Matt's dad helped Dev out and eased him to the ground.

Scout was on his side, his eyes still open but not focusing on anything. Matt leaned over him, smoothing the fur on his head. Scout didn't even seem to register that Matt was there. He just stared into the distance. Matt couldn't tell if he was breathing.

"Scout!" Matt said desperately. "Please, Scout, it's me. It's me, Matt."

Nothing.

"Scout, please!" Matt choked back a sob. "Can you hear me?"

"Matt—"

Matt pressed his lips to Scout's ear. "Buddy," he pleaded in a distressed whisper. "I know you can hear me. You're going to be okay. Just hang in there."

Matt's whole body was shaking. He thought about all the times Scout had come back for him, or risked his own life, or slept on the floor by Matt's bed and woken him up with a giant wet slurp across the face. A fat tear slid down Matt's cheek.

"Matt."

Matt looked up, as if he were hearing his dad for the first time.

"I don't know if Scout is going to make it, buddy," his dad said, choking up as he spoke.

Matt squeezed his eyes shut, as if that would stop his dad's words from being true.

"Matt . . ." Dev was right next to him.

"It's okay, Matt." Amaiya was on his other side. Curtis stood right behind him.

"Please," Matt begged. "Please—we have to try to help him! We can't just leave him here."

Matt's dad studied his son's tearstained face. With

a grim nod, his dad gingerly lowered himself onto the rocks, flinching at the pain in his ankle. He positioned himself over Scout and placed both hands, one on top of the other, on the dog's rib cage.

Matt stayed close to Scout's side. The other kids stepped back, giving them space. Curtis looked down at his hands, then at the rocks and trees. Dev was stone-faced. Amaiya buried her face in her hands.

Holding his elbows straight, Matt's dad pushed down hard on Scout's chest in a series of fifteen quick compressions.

"Hold his mouth shut," Matt's dad directed. "Breathe once into his nostrils—hard."

Matt wrapped both hands around Scout's muzzle and placed his mouth over his nose. He blew with all the power he could muster from his aching lungs.

"Good." Matt's dad performed another round of compressions, and Matt repeated the breathing maneuver.

For a torturously long moment, there was nothing. They did it again. And again.

Suddenly, after the fourth round of CPR, Scout grunted loudly and sucked in a huge gulp of air. He coughed and spit up a few mouthfuls of water.

"Scout!" Matt cried. "You're alive!"

Scout raised his head and blinked at Matt. He dropped his head back onto the rocks and began to breathe in a fast, choppy rhythm.

Matt let out a sob of relief. The others sniffled and wiped their eyes with the backs of their hands.

"Matt," his dad said gently, "Scout needs to get to a vet right away. And I need to get you kids home in one piece. Those helicopters didn't see us, but they put out the fire on this side. It's safe to head down the mountain on our own now. We need to move out."

"Okay, Dad." Matt took a few steadying breaths.

"Can you carry him?" Matt's dad gestured at Scout. "I'm sorry I can't do it, buddy, but my ankle—"

"It's okay, Dad," Matt said. "I've got him." Matt slid his arms under Scout. He gently lifted him and draped the dog over his shoulders.

Matt felt Scout breathing against the back of his neck. Holding Scout's legs in either hand and fighting tears, Matt looked around at the others.

"Let's go home."

20

THEY TREKKED THROUGH A CHARRED WASTELAND.

The ground was a blackened layer as far as the eye could see. Pine trees and sagebrush were bare and scorched—nothing but skeletons of dead wood. Even the rocks looked like charcoal. A heavy blanket of soot and ash covered the still-smoldering landscape. Smoke seemed to rise from deep inside a heartbroken Earth.

They headed toward the trail that would lead them back to the bottom of the mountain. Dev leaned heavily on Amaiya as he walked. Matt's dad had an arm over Curtis's shoulders. He hopped and limped down the hill, with Curtis steadying him every time he swayed.

The farther they traveled downhill, the farther they moved from the lingering mass of smoke that still blocked out the sun.

The world around them was silent. No birds sang in the trees. No lizards skittered under rocks. No bears crunched through the bushes.

Nobody spoke.

After a few minutes, Matt's ears popped with the change in elevation.

Matt barely noticed. He couldn't have cared less about their surroundings or how far they had traveled. All he cared about was Scout, who sagged heavily across his shoulders. Matt reached up and laid his hand on Scout's chest. It was rising and falling, but it still hadn't settled into an even rhythm. Matt didn't like the way it felt—something wasn't right.

Matt fought the fear that threatened to overcome him. He focused only on his dog's shallow breathing and the sound of his own footsteps.

Every step forward brought him closer to help for Scout.

Matt barely noticed when his dad stopped moving and, leaning on Curtis, tugged open his pocket and pulled out his phone. Matt and Bridget had often teased their dad for always insisting on a fully water-proof phone case, but for once, Matt wasn't laughing.

His dad swiped at his phone screen and waited. "Finally," he said to himself. "Service." He dialed quickly.

As if from a hundred miles away, Matt heard his dad talking to his mom. "Honey, it's good to hear your voice. Matt's okay—he's fine. We're all okay. Yeah. See you at the bottom. Send an ambulance. Dev and I are going to need medical attention STAT. No, don't worry. We're fine." He shot Matt a sideways look and lowered his voice. "But Scout . . . I don't know. I really just . . . don't know."

Matt felt the ground even out beneath his feet. The slope flattened as they got closer to the bottom. He picked up his pace, moving faster and faster, until he was practically running down the hill.

He was the first to set foot in the parking lot, where he and the others were immediately swarmed by EMTs and National Guard troops bearing Mylar blankets and bottles of water. Matt hardly noticed them.

"Matt!" The sound of his mom's voice brought him back to the present. The bubble around Matt popped, and suddenly he saw the world in color again, heard the rapid chatter of dozens of rescue workers swarming around, and felt a soft morning breeze on his skin.

But one single thought blared like a siren in Matt's brain: *Scout needs help*.

"Oh thank God! Matt—" His mom fought tears. "I'm so glad you're here." She wrapped Matt in a tight embrace and rested her cheek on Scout's head. "We've been trying to get to you all night, but it was just too dangerous. The conditions kept changing. But I knew if the water helicopters could put out the fire, you guys could get yourselves down safely." She hugged him even tighter. "I am so incredibly angry at you and so incredibly happy to see you."

"Mom—" Matt's voice cracked with emotion.

She held him at arm's length and looked him over from head to toe. "Are you okay? Are you hurt? Anywhere?"

"Mom, please—" Matt took a few quick breaths through his nose and waited until he knew he could speak again. "I'm fine. But—I don't know if Scout's okay. He needs help. Mom, please help him . . ."

It was no use fighting it. Matt let the hot tears spill from his eyes and roll down his cheeks.

One of the men tried to lift Scout from Matt's

shoulders, but his mom held up her hand. "It's okay, soldier. I've got this." She pulled Matt over to a gurney.

Matt's mom lifted Scout from his shoulders, and together they gently lowered the dog onto the flat surface. Scout barely moved. Matt's mom took Scout's head in her hands and pulled open his eyelids, then let them close again. She placed a hand on the inside of his back thigh, feeling his pulse, and counted as she looked at her watch.

She put a hand on Scout's heart and left it there. "Matt," she said, her voice soft. Matt knew from her tone what she wanted to say to him. He bit his lip and looked away. *"Matt."* She took her son's face in her hands and turned his head toward her. "It doesn't look good, sweetheart. I know how much you've just been through, but I want to prepare you for what could happen."

There was a hard lump in Matt's throat, and he felt sad in every inch, every cell of his body. He had never known that being heartbroken meant you felt it from the soles of your feet to the top of your scalp.

"But if Scout has any chance, then we need to get

him to the vet right this second. Are you willing to leave your dad and all your friends here?"

Matt looked around the parking lot. Dev was rattling by on a stretcher, a plastic mask covering his mouth and nose. Mist rose from holes in the mask, which was connected to a long tube extending from a small machine that lay across his legs. He was inhaling the medicine that would open up his airways instantly. Dev had his head back and his eyes closed, but there was color in his cheeks again. His parents were on one side, and his older sister, Gita, was on the other.

Amaiya's parents and Curtis's mom were there too, holding their kids in fierce embraces, as if they would never let go again.

Matt's dad was in the back of an ambulance, with an IV tube dangling above his arm. An EMT examined his ankle. Matt and his dad locked eyes. His dad smiled and mouthed one word at him: *Go*.

Thanks, Matt mouthed back. He turned to his mom. "Let's go."

His mom nodded. "Major," she called out to a man across the lot. He jogged over. "You're in charge." The man gave a quick salute and got back to work.

Matt and his mom wheeled Scout over to her truck and eased him into the back seat. Matt climbed in next to the dog and gently stroked his head. Scout's eyes were closed, and his nostrils flared slightly with every weak breath. Matt focused on that tiny movement as a sign of hope.

21

HIS MOM STEERED THE SPEEDING SUV down the highway, weaving between cars and racing back to town. As they drove, Matt rubbed the soft spot under Scout's chin and stared out the window as the mountains and rocks flashed by.

They called ahead, and when his mom screeched into the parking lot of the emergency veterinary hospital, two vet technicians came running through the automatic doors, pushing a stretcher.

"On three!" one of the techs said. On her count, they slid Scout off the seat and lifted him onto the gurney. Matt jogged after them. The metal cart rattled and clanked as they ran back across the parking lot and burst through the doors. Matt watched, helpless, as the vet ran out from a back room, lifting her stethoscope from her neck and pressing it to Scout's chest while the techs shouted information at her. They ran as a unit toward an exam room and hurtled through the door, which swallowed them instantly.

The waiting room was suddenly empty and still. Animal Planet blared from a television mounted high up on a wall.

Matt stood in the middle of the room, unsure what to do with himself. His mom guided him toward a chair, and suddenly his legs turned to jelly. He collapsed into the seat and bent forward, resting his arms and head on his knees. His mom sat next to him, lightly rubbing his back.

The TV shouted. Phones rang. Computers dinged and vets whispered behind the receptionist's desk.

But Matt didn't hear any of it. All he heard were the three words that formed a steady drumbeat in his head.

Will Scout live?

"Buddy"—Matt's mom tapped his knee—"I know you're exhausted, but there's something I want to tell you."

"I know, Mom. I'm in serious trouble. It's okay. I deserve it."

"No, honey, that's not it."

He raised his eyes to meet hers. "What is it, then?"

She gathered her thoughts for a moment. "Matt, you are so incredibly brave. And I am so proud of you—your dad and I both are."

"Thanks, Mom."

"But," she went on, lovingly taking his chin in her hand and turning his head toward hers, "you know you don't have to run up burning mountains or rescue little kids from floods in order for us to feel that way."

Matt couldn't help but laugh. It did sound kind of crazy when she put it that way, but he'd just been trying to do what he thought was right. "I know that, Mom."

"I'm glad to hear it. It's just that—" She paused and watched cars whiz by outside the window for a moment.

"It's just what?" Matt prodded her.

She let out a long sigh. "It's just that I don't want you to feel like you have to be like me and Dad— because of what we do for a living. You don't have to live up to some ideal of us."

Matt turned her words over in his mind. "I'm not sure what you mean."

"Your dad and I . . . we really love what we do."

"I know."

"And we're really lucky that we get to help people—it's a huge honor. I wouldn't want to do anything else with my life. Except be your mom, of course. But you're still young, Matt. You're an amazing person, even if you decide you just want to be . . . you know . . . a regular kid." She took his hand and threaded her fingers through his. "You don't have to put yourself at risk to be a good person, is all I'm saying."

Matt replayed the events of the past twenty-four hours in his mind. He remembered how he had felt when he heard that his friends might be in danger—and the powerful instinct he had to *do* something.

An instinct to help.

He remembered how he had felt after he commanded Scout to stand down when they were face-to-face with the bear. He thought back to how Scout's whole body shook when they were trapped by the smoke, and how his dog had calmed down when Matt held him close. And he remembered the unbelievable feeling of laying eyes on his friends in the cave—and knowing they were all safe.

"But, Mom," Matt said, "what if I *am* like you and

Dad—and Scout? What if helping people is what I love to do too?"

"Well," she said with a sigh, "then you can't fight who you are. So we'll just have to show you the ropes. And teach you how to stay out of trouble."

She pulled him into a hug, and the arm of the chair dug into his ribs.

"Sounds good," Matt said into her shoulder.

"Now I know how my mother felt," his mom laughed into his hair.

They sat like that for a while until the reality of where they were—and why—sank back in. Matt sat up. "Mom?"

"Yes, honey?"

"What . . . If . . . What—" His voice quavered. "What if Scout doesn't make it?"

She didn't answer. Instead she took his hand and held it tightly.

By the time the vet stepped out of the back and walked across the cold tile floor of the waiting room, Matt had accepted that the worst was going to happen.

His mom stood up, but Matt couldn't bring himself

to get out of his seat. He looked up at the vet's face, and what he saw there surprised him.

She was smiling.

Matt jumped up. "Is he going to make it?"

"He is," the vet said. "He is one lucky dog. You got him here just in time."

"Thank you," Matt's mom said through tears. "Thank you so much."

"You're welcome. Scout is a real trooper. He fought to survive." She reached out and put a hand on Matt's shoulder. "And I have a feeling that's because he knew there were some pretty important people out here cheering him on."

"Can I see him?"

The vet and Matt's mom exchanged a glance. His mom nodded.

"Sure. This way."

Matt and his mom followed the vet into a large room divided into smaller areas by curtains. At the back of the room, Scout lay on a bed. Tubes and cords protruded from what seemed like every part of his body. Machines blipped and beeped, and an IV dripped slowly into a clear tube attached to Scout's leg.

Matt stood by his head. Scout was under heavy anesthesia and had an oxygen mask over his muzzle. He breathed deeply and slowly.

Matt reached out a hand but stopped. He looked over at the vet.

"It's okay," she said. "You can pet him. He'll appreciate it."

Matt stroked Scout's neck and leaned down to whisper in his ear.

"Hi, Scout," Matt said softly. "It's me."

At the sound of Matt's voice, Scout fluttered his eyelids, but he was too groggy to open them all the way.

"It's okay—you just rest. I'll be here when you wake up."

Scout closed his eyes.

Matt's mom put a hand on Scout's belly. "Scout . . ." Her voice welled with emotion and she took a deep breath. "Scout, we're going to get you home as soon as we can. This family wouldn't be the same without you, you know."

"Thanks for saving us today," Matt said.

Scout managed to open his eyes just enough to look up at Matt.

"Hey, buddy," Matt said quietly.

Scout opened his mouth as much as he could inside the mask and let out a hoarse bark.

Matt and his mom broke out into huge grins, tears spilling from their eyes.

Matt wrapped his arms around Scout as tightly as he dared and buried his face in his silky fur.

"It's okay, Scout," Matt said. "You're going to come home."

22

THE WATER RAN BROWN INTO the bathtub drain.

"Jeez, Scout! How can you still be dirty?" Matt dumped more dog shampoo into his palm and lathered up Scout's fur. It was his third bath since he'd come home from the vet. Scout sat patiently, a pouf of suds sitting atop his head like a crown.

Matt's dad stuck his head in the bathroom door. "It took me about a dozen showers to feel clean." Leaning on his crutches, he raised the giant cast that ran from his toes to his knee in the air. "And I can't even scrub all of me yet." He hobbled into the room and sat down on the edge of the tub.

Scout wagged his tail in the water, sending a spray of soapy water onto both of them.

"Scout!" Matt laughed, wiping his face on his sleeve.

"Good thing you're still recovering, Scout," Matt's dad joked, "or I'd get you for that one."

Matt leaned in and pressed his nose to Scout's wet snout. Scout licked his chin. "Don't worry, buddy," Matt said. "Dad's all talk."

"Not true! I'm tough as nails," Matt's dad said. "But still not as tough as you, Scout."

Even the vet was amazed at how quickly Scout had recovered from smoke inhalation, a near drowning, burned paws, a showdown with a bear, and a dozen other little injuries. But he was one tough dog.

"Dad, when will you learn that Scout is stronger than all four of us combined?"

A funny look crossed his dad's face.

"What?" Matt asked.

"Nothing." His dad sounded a little choked up. "It's just—well, I've actually learned a lot these past few days. About this dog. About my family. About life."

"Like what?"

His dad thought for a moment. "Well," he began,

"actually, there's one thing I think we both learned in the past few days, Matt. Up on that mountain, in fact."

"What's that?"

His dad raised an eyebrow. "I learned that it's hard to be brave enough to do the right thing."

Matt looked away from his dad. He ran a wet hand down Scout's slippery back. Even though everyone was safe—and his dad and Scout were going to make full recoveries—Matt still felt sick to his stomach for dragging them into such a dangerous situation. But he was going to have to learn to live with that feeling—and to use it to motivate himself to do better next time.

"Yeah," Matt said after a moment. "You're right. It really is hard."

Matt reached for the spray nozzle and turned on the water, checking the temperature before he rinsed the bubbles off Scout's fur.

"Matt-o," his dad said, "my wings have been clipped for the time being." His dad gestured at his cast. "But sooner or later I'll be back on both feet, and I'll ship out again."

"I know, Dad. And I promise not to do anything stupid while you're gone."

"Actually I was thinking just the opposite."

"What do you mean?"

"I learned something else on that mountain, pal."

"What's that?"

Matt tilted his head to the side as he listened.

"I learned that you have serious guts, Matt-o. I mean, I knew it before, but this time I *saw* it. You figured out what the right thing was—maybe a little late—but regardless, you figured it out, and you did it."

Matt didn't know what to say. He didn't feel like he had been the brave one compared to his dad, and Dev, and Scout, and Amaiya, and Curtis.

"Now, maybe next time," his dad went on, "you could work on figuring it out just a tad faster. What do you say?"

"Sure, Dad." Matt grinned from ear to ear. "I'll see what I can do about that."

"But in the meantime, I know that while I'm gone, I can rest easy, because you, and this guy"—he leaned over and scratched Scout's soapy head—"will be here. And together, you'll keep us all in pretty good hands."

"Thanks, Dad. I promise to always look out for our family."

"Guys, dinner's ready!" Bridget called up from the kitchen. Matt's mom walked by the bathroom door, headed downstairs. She rapped twice on the doorframe as she passed. "Rinse off that filthy dog and come eat," she said.

"Yessir," Matt's dad said, saluting.

Matt started to rinse off Scout. The water finally ran clear. He thought about all the soot and dirt that had been lodged deep in Scout's coat, and where it had come from. He thought about how much danger they had faced up on Mount Kit—and how scared he had been. He thought about how awful he had felt not knowing if his friends—his best friends—were safe, and how incredible it felt to find them. He thought about how grateful he was that his dad had gone on this mission with him in the first place, and that Scout had been there to save his life. He thought about how amazing it had felt to see his mom at the bottom of the mountain.

"I learned something too," Matt said.

"Yeah? What's that?"

Matt scratched Scout under the chin and turned to look his dad squarely in the eye. "That I'm the luckiest guy on Earth."

23

DEV'S PHONE DINGED IN HIS BACK POCKET. He looked at it and groaned.

"Your mom again?" Matt asked, snapping his bike lock shut.

"Yup." Dev shook his head. "It's eight in the morning. I left the house less than ten minutes ago."

"Aw, she's just worried about her Devvy," Matt ribbed him.

"Well," Dev said, "Devvy wants to tell her she has nothing to worry about." Dev recited his reply text as he tapped it out. "Yes. I. Have. My. Inhaler. All. Good." Dev groaned and stuffed the phone back in his pocket.

Amaiya hopped off her bike while it was still in motion. "Your mom?"

"His mom," Curtis confirmed from his spot by the bike rack.

The four of them adjusted their backpacks and stared up at their school. The principal stood at the top of the steps, waving them in.

"We survived a wildfire and Ms. Fagan can't even let us be one minute late." Dev sighed.

"Back to normal," Amaiya grumbled.

They headed toward the building.

"So what're we doing this weekend?" Curtis asked with a yawn. "What? It's never too early to plan ahead."

"Hiking?" Dev replied with a too-big grin.

The others groaned.

"I think you've been banned from all hiking trails in the state of Nevada," Matt shot back. "But actually, I have a better idea."

Dev, Amaiya, and Curtis stopped in their tracks and turned to face Matt. "What's that?" they asked all at once.

"Movie night," Matt said with a little shrug. "My house. Pizza. Popcorn. Scout. I thought we could do something nice and safe for once."

"You've never invited us over to your house!" Dev said, throwing his arms up in excitement and dancing a goofy jig.

"I'm in," Curtis said.

"Sounds fun, Matt," Amaiya said, her nose wrinkling as she smiled. "Especially if Scout will be there."

"Great," Matt said, looking from Amaiya to Curtis to Dev.

Seeing their groggy faces in the early morning sunlight—like he did every day—it was hard for Matt to believe that he'd ever questioned what they were made of. Up on that mountain, his friends had put themselves on the line for each other—and for him. They'd shown him who they were, all right, and he would never doubt them again.

"Movies, pizza, and Scout." Matt grinned. "I can't wait."

ACKNOWLEDGMENTS

This book is about family, friendship, teamwork, kindness, helping others—and, of course, dogs. In other words, all the good things in life.

Brian and the goons—how do I thank you for being absolutely everything? JiffyD! Virginia Wing—thank you for being our rock of Gigi. Kunsang Bhuti and Tenzin Dekyi, thank you for your loving care.

Kristen Ardigo, Stacey Silverman, Halina Siwolop, Brent Rice, Laurie Maher, Alexandra Loxton, Charles Loxton, Ellen Marmur, Lindsay Barrett, Lisa Wilson, Verena Wiesendanger, and Caitlin Travers—thank you for being so tried-and-true. I'd climb a flaming mountain for you!

Go, Team Scout! Les Morgenstein, Josh Bank, and Sara Shandler at Alloy, and Margaret Anastas and the amazing Luana Horry at Harper—you guys are best in show. Thank you for being Hero and Scout's biggest fans. Thanks always to the sales, marketing, and publicity groups at Harper, and to Katelyn Hales at the Robin Straus Agency.

And thank you to the team captains: Robin Straus, a tireless champion; Romy Golan, so kind . . . so patient; and Hayley Wagreich, always my favorite editor—we (by "we" I mean "you") did it.

And finally: Rescue dogs rule! Our wicked Vida is a source of such joy—and many funny dog mannerisms. Thanks to Animal Lighthouse Rescue (alrcares.com) and all the rescue organizations for saving so many dogs and enriching the lives of so many families.

Love dogs?
You may also like...

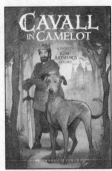

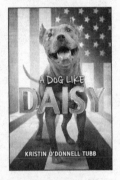

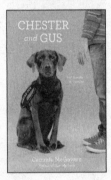

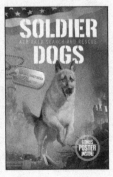